Well, he's been around the world in a plane and half way round the world in a ship.

He has never spoken to a king, but has passed the time of day with a pauper or two.

And of all the countries he has visited and people he has chewed the fat with has arrived at the conclusion that the basic needs of a king or pauper are similar; the difference being one of accessibility.

Likewise, in the job that he was associated with over many years, he had access to CEO's and first line supervisors, helping their organisation achieve whatever kept them in business.

This type of exposure has given the author a mine of material to call on, in a sometimes controversial way, but always with good humour.

This book is dedicated to, Lavinia Ivy Arbery and Sean Arbery.

Jim Arbery

A TALE OF TWO PIXIES

Living in a Quasi-world

AUSTIN MACAULEY PUBLISHERS™
LONDON * CAMBRIDGE * NEW YORK * SHARJAH

Copyright © Jim Arbery 2023

The right of Jim Arbery to be identified as author of this work has been asserted by the author in accordance with sections 77 and 78 of the Copyright, Designs and Patents Act 1988.

All rights reserved. No part of this publication may be reproduced, stored in a retrieval system or transmitted in any form or by any means, electronic, mechanical, photocopying, recording or otherwise, without the prior permission of the publishers.

Any person who commits any unauthorised act in relation to this publication may be liable to criminal prosecution and civil claims for damages.

This is a work of fiction. Names, characters, businesses, places, events, locales and incidents are either the products of the author's imagination or used in a fictitious manner. Any resemblance to actual persons, living or dead, or actual events is purely coincidental.

A CIP catalogue record for this title is available from the British Library.

ISBN 9781398409293 (Paperback)
ISBN 9781398409309 (ePub e-book)

www.austinmacauley.com

First Published 2023
Austin Macauley Publishers Ltd®
1 Canada Square
Canary Wharf
London
E14 5AA

My thanks to the staff of Austin Macauuley for their help, guidance and patience. Also, I would like to thank humankind for their behaviour, without which this book could not have been written.

Synopsis

If you have the ability to imagine, you hold the key to another world.

Once upon a time, there were two pixies that set out to create good will for the much-maligned mythological world.

They may not be the sort of pixies you have at the bottom of your garden, but fairy tales have the reputation for being deceptive.

There is often an unseen sleight of hand, slip of the tongue, an invisible presence, a wizard in the offing, a young woman or youth in distress and always a knight on a mighty steed, with a hoarse voice.

All right, so what have we got so far?

Well, what we have are two scallywag pixies, one with whitish blond hair and mesmerising mauve eyes, the other has dark brown hair and startling green eyes.

Both a smidgen over knee height, they are usually wearing jeans polo shirt and sneakers, with a smart phone in their back pocket.

So, there you have it, simple as that…

Author

A Walk in the Park

The pixies approached the bus shelter as the rain decided to recreate itself to a misty drizzle, thinking it was strange that would be passengers were not sheltering in a facility built for their ease and comfort.

As the pixies got closer, a bus pulled up, the people boarded and were whisked on their way to whatever chance intended for them, on a cool and windy day.

As M & D came abreast of the shelter they peered into its depths and began to understand the commuter's reluctance to wait there in, it contained a street person lying prone on the bench seat, snoring loudly.

There is no nice way of putting it the odour that wafted towards the pixies was almost visible in its potency, causing them to retreat a metre or so.

"Well," said Mixie, her mauve eyes twinkling, "an example of a man not enjoying good fortune, what do you think of that, Dixie?"

Before her companion could reply, the old man sat up and proceeded to perform what was obviously a well-practiced ritual.

He took off his greasy stained cap, then scratched his head, whereupon small white flakes settled on his shoulders like driven snow.

After a thoughtful pause he stroked his patchy beard, belched heavily, thereby encouraging the pixies to move even further back.

At which stage, a short hiatus took place, before a movement occurred which involved the dishevelled old man (DOM) gripping the edge of the seat with both hands and emitting a thunderous noise; startling the pixies enough for them to retire to the roof of the bus shelter.

Here they awaited the dispersal of toxins…

The silence that followed was interrupted by a sound that could only be described as slurping, enticing the pixies to take a peek.

What they saw was a bottle that contained a bluish liquid accompanied by an echoing belch.

The pixies exchanged a glance, with Dixie saying, "It's the first time I have seen yellow, red and blue eyes."

She nodded. "Yeah, jaundiced I would say."

Venturing once again at the entrance, the DOM caught sight of the intrepid duo, saying, "Where did you two come from, the police?"

"We, sir," said Mixie, indignantly, "are pixies!"

The DOM's laugh was wet with a touch of phlegm, as he said, "Pull the other one, it's got bells on it."

"We would rather not," said Dixie, "pulling your other leg may be at the risk of further emissions."

Slurp, slurp, belch, was the DOM's reply.

Ever curious about *Homo sapiens* and their self-destructive behaviour, Mixie said, "What brought you to this sorry state, sir?"

There was a long silence, whilst the blue rinsed brain cells of the DOM considered Mixie's question, finally he said, "Do you want the truth or the story I tell?"

The pixies laughed, before Dixie said, "We would rather have the truth because the story would probably sound like a fairy tale."

Looking past the pixies, the DOM said, thoughtfully, "We lost our business in a gigantic scam…"

He paused, took a slug from his bottle, then continued, "Things happened, I took to the drink, my wife and I drifted apart, then…" The DOM became silent.

Shrewdly, Mixie said, "Hmm that, sounds like a possibility."

The DOM sighed, shrugged, slurped yet again, having nothing further to say.

"Whatever you do, Mixie, don't strike a match it could be dangerous," said her partner, as his green eyes met the mauve.

Just then, a bus drew alongside the shelter, slowing, the driver peered, decided there were no customers and continued on his way.

She smiled. "My name is Mixie, and this is my partner, Dixie, what is your name?"

Speaking to himself more than anyone else, the DOM murmured, "I should know this, um, give me a moment."

The pixies were silent, listening and observing was something they were good at.

Eventually, after another slurp, the bus shelter gentleman, said decisively, "Claude, yes, I'm sure it's Claude."

"Well, Claude," said Mixie, "how would you like a new start?"

"What was that?" said the old man on the brink of oblivion, and well aware of it.

"Mixie and I can get hold of clean second-hand clothing from the skin out, including shoes," said Dixie.

Claude was silent, thinking, looking down at the flip flops on his feet... "Could the shoes be brown?" he asked.

"Absolutely," said Mixie, "but!"

Claude's eyes swam about in his head, before he croaked, "But what?"

Her voice firm, she said, "The terms are these Claude, we get you the gear, you go to the City Mission and scrub yourself from head to toe and back again, put on your new stuff and meet us afterwards."

The chance in a lifetime old man thought about the terms of endearment, before saying, "Okay, we could meet in, Albert Park."

The pixies eyes met, "Right," said Dixie, "where in Albert Park and what time?"

After a long thoughtful silence, Claude said, "Use the entrance by the university, you'll see me, at midnight."

"It's a deal," said, the pixies, in unison, "shake on it."

And that's what they did, with the old man's grip being surprisingly strong.

***

The pixies approached the park and saw immediately where Claude had decided to sit.

As they got close to the now smartly dressed, minus the bottle, clean shaven old man, Mixie said, "There's something odd going on here, Dixie."

"Hmm, I agree," he said, as his partner checked Claude's vital signs.

Shaking her head, she murmured, "He's gone."

"Yes indeed, for a walk in the park," said Dixie.

***

Life Is a Beach

Several days after their sad encounter with the homeless man, the pixies paid a visit to a beautiful beach they had heard of.

The bay was traditional, its shape a scimitar, and more than likely took thousands of years to form.

At first glance flawless golden sand embraced by Pohutukawa trees in full blossom, a natural phenomenon of exquisite beauty.

From the depths of one of the, so called, Christmas trees, the pixies took in the scene before them…

He looked at her, she at him. "Not many people here," said Dixie.

"Hmm," she murmured, lazily, "this place is a bit off the map, you know."

"Yeah, and the everlasting road works would put people off," he added.

A gentle breeze disturbed the brilliant crimson petals of the Pohutukawa causing some of them to fall and add to the magic carpet beneath each tree.

Mixie gently touched a flower. "Problem is, Dixie, some of the people that do make their way here, are…" She took a breath, sighed, fell silent held his hand.

He whispered in her ear completing her thought.

Shaking her head, she laughed. "That is unprintable, Dixie, but true."

Looking to the far end of the bay, where time and tide had formed a low headland meeting the beach, Dixie said, "Do we go and help?"

She nodded. "Yes, why not, good idea, looks like they've picked up plenty of garbage, even at this early hour."

"It's the condoms, needles and glass that are the biggest problem, apparently," he said.

She nodded. "Yeah, and don't forget the cigarette butts."

As the pixies busied themselves helping to clear the beach of toxic waste, a woman some distance away, said to her companion, pointing, "Look, what are those cute little creatures over there?"

He peered, squinting against the morning sun, shading his eyes with his hand. "Dollars to doughnuts, they are some kind of drone."

She frowned. "They don't look very mechanical to me."

Straightening his back with a groan, the man smiled, knowingly. "The techs these days can do anything."

"Yes, I suppose so," she said. Stooping once again, she whispered, "Let's move closer, just slowly and see if we can get a good look at them."

"Good idea," he said, "they won't notice if we're nonchalant about it."

"Oh, big words this morning, Phil, nonchalant, it must be all this fresh air."

The couple moved slowly but surely, with the pixies, apparently, unaware.

After a moment or two, she said, "That's strange."

"What now, Doris, we can't just run over, can we?"

"It's not that," she said, "we move closer, they don't appear to move, but the distance remains the same."

"I know what's happening," he said, authoritatively, with a touch of misplaced masculine misinformation.

Doris sniffed. "Okay, what is it, clever clogs?"

He pointed towards the headland. "Take a look, there's a group of people up there, I bet one of them is in control of those two drones and playing silly buggers with us."

"I can't see any control panel, with those toggle thingy's, Phil."

He nodded, knowingly. "It won't be that; someone will be using a smart phone to control their movements."

She smiled. "Yes, of course, there's always a logical answer, after all, we're not in fairy land, well done, Phil."

He glowed inwardly and modestly at the recognition of his precise thinking and rat trap brain.

In the meantime, picking up a ciggy butt and popping it into a plastic bag, Mixie said, "I think we are being watched."

He nodded. "Yeah, I think you're right... Watch out, Mixie, there's a piece of glass right in front of you!"

She stepped back. "Damn, you know, Dixie, life at times can be a bit of a beach."

"Did you say beach?" he asked.

Sometime later on their way back to town, with Doris and Phil frustratingly none the wiser the pixies came across a cow stuck in a ditch, hmm...

"We should help that poor animal, Dixie," she said.

Dixie looked at the cow with a critical eye. "Well firstly, the animal looks large to me, also grumpy and bad tempered."

Shaking her head in disbelief, she said, "If you were up to your backside in mud, your disposition would be even worse."

"Yeah, I suppose so," he said reluctantly.

She gave him a hard stare. "We can't leave her; besides, several cars have passed and no one is interested in helping."

With an exaggerated sigh of resignation, he said, "Okay, but we need to have a plan."

"Of course, we need to have a plan," she agreed, "what is it?"

Their discussion became heated, with Mixie insisting upon taking the front end because of her new white jeans, meaning, in nautical terms, her beloved got the aft of the beast.

For their size, pixies are very strong, but even so, after a great deal of pushing, tugging and cajoling the cow insisted on remaining in the ditch.

Puffing and panting the pixies sat on top of a nearby five barred gate, looking down on the cow that expected to be rescued.

"We need another plan," she said, thoughtfully, as both sat there chewing a piece of straw and cogitating.

Their eyes met, both smiled, as Mixie shouted, "Bribery, it works every time!"

And that's what they did, with clumps of grass held at a tempting distance, the cow, who they had named, Daisy (what else?), extricated herself.

However, the aftermath was something else, with Mixie complaining bitterly that her jeans were ruined and even worse, she had broken a nail.

Dixie also cheerfully reminded her of the naughty language she had used to encourage the useless cow to pitch in and help.

Upon reaching home base they stood for seventeen steaming minutes under the shower, with Mixie yelling, "I don't care about using lots of hot water, Dixie."

"She doesn't mean that," shouted her partner, to no one in particular.

He got a poke in the ribs.

An afterthought from the pixies:

The stuff of life often comes unstuck at the edges.

A stitch is dropped.

One's view of the world bent as if looking through a prism.
With kind regards from Mixie and Dixie.

***

Pixie Chatter and Random Thoughts

Several days before their encounter with the bus shelter gentleman, their visit to the beach, and the cow in the ditch escapade, the pixies had been elsewhere…

"Did you know, Dixie," she said, thoughtfully, "it's amazing how technology has made humungous advances since the invention of candy floss, whilst basic human behaviour, not so much…but, of course, I could be wrong."

The pixies were well hidden, sitting astride a branch of a tall leafy tree in one of the many public reserves in the city.

The weather was typical of an iffy summer with grey sky, warm, with humidity muggy.

Families were scattered hither and yon with their barbeques, people of all shapes, sizes and colour playing a variety of games; skateboarders were skilfully missing pedestrians on footpaths and giving old people a fright…

A human scene the pixies never tired of witnessing.

"So, Dixie, what do you think of my latest theory?" she asked.

He frowned, searching for an answer, as a man some distance away stabbed a sausage in the back… "Yes, there is no doubt about technology, then again, there's chewing gum to add to the list."

"Yeah," she said, continuing to create an intertwined cradle of leaves filched from their host.

A peaceful tranquil silence enveloped the pixies, like filmy gossamer, as they gazed upon the tableau of human activity unfolding before them.

Mixie broke the silence, by saying, "You know, Dixie, I still maintain human behaviour hasn't changed much since I've been around."

Scratching his head, which helped him to think, he said, "Where are we going with this?"

"It puzzles me" – she shrugged, pulled a face – "is what I'm saying."

A zephyr on its way north stirred the leaves, birds sent tweets, kids bellowed in the face of their friends lest they not be heard, the world continued to spin despite human activity.

Dixie shifted his position and wriggled himself comfortable once again. "Your point being?"

Her mauve eyes swept over him. "Well, every year it seems to be here we go again."

He nodded, watched a leaf fall, try to spin its way to the centre of the earth, stopped only by the earth itself. "You mean people are still disagreeing about almost everything unless you agree with them, and kill each other in the process?"

"And don't forget there are still millions of people without the basics of life," Mixie added, as she placed her woven basket in the crook of a branch.

He looked at her, raised an eyebrow. "So what are you going to do about it?"

She sighed, shrugged. "Put the problem in the too hard basket, same as always."

He squeezed her hand. "That doesn't sound like you Mixie, saying there is nothing to be done."

A smile played on her lips and she didn't notice two birds that were eavesdropping, as she whispered in Dixie's ear.

He listened, a pixie moment drifted by, nodding, he said, "Yeah, that would work."

***

As the pixies sat quietly contemplating Mixie's suggestion, Dixie's attention drifted to a family directly below their vantage point, three children, parents and a large cat.

Breaking into her personal thoughts about humanities future, Dixie said, "That's a pretty swish barbeque they've got down there."

Mixie's eyes drifted to the group making preparations for lunch. "Yes, stainless steel, portable with wheels, gas bottle and attached foldable table, it would have cost a heap."

A pixie moment ticked by.

"What do you think of the cat?" he asked. "It's bigger than our furry sweetheart."

"That lump is enormous…bigger than us…and a lovely colour," she said.

"Yeah, what is that colour?"

She thought for a moment. "I think it is called tawny, a reddish brown, beautiful and the cat is not tethered, it just sits there looking on."

"Yes, waiting patiently for a sausage," he said.

"Yeah," she grinned, "there's no doubt about *Homo sapiens*, they love their sausages, big greasy eye popping bangers."

Dixie let out a stifled guffaw which went unnoticed by the bipeds but was picked up by the cat.

With a flick of its tail, one bound and a squiggle the cat was sitting opposite the pixies fixing them with a malicious squinty glare.

"Come back," shouted the woman, "come back, Matilda, don't you dare touch any birds."

Matilda, however, had found something far more interesting than dry as dust birds...

The man laughed. "She'll be right back in a tick when I wave a sausage at her."

"Well," said Mixie, "if a cat can look at a king, pixies can look at a cat."

Matilda's eyes went big and round, the creatures opposite her were certainly strange looking birds and what's more were able to speak.

"Nice pussy," said Dixie, putting out a tentative hand, which Matilda sniffed, deciding immediately that it wasn't human, even if it looked similar.

"Try smoothing Matilda's head, Dixie," Mixie suggested, with a naughty grin.

"No way!" he said. "You do it, look at the size of her paws and those claws digging into that branch."

"I noticed." She giggled.

A pixie moment ticked by...

There was a shout, as a huge dog came bounding out of nowhere, growling and heading straight for the expensive barbeque and its contents.

The man and woman stood in front of their children as the barbeque was knocked flying with glistening sausages performing a graceful pas de deux before gravity took charge...

There was shouting and screaming with people scattering every which way.

One instant Matilda was sitting opposite the pixies, the next she had hurled herself in one bound onto the dogs back, claws hooking in like crampons, as her teeth sank into a floppy right ear.

Mixie leaned forward with interest. "Hmm, that cat is probably right pawed," she murmured. "Wow, I'm glad it's the dog and not us."

"Jeez," came from Dixie, "I think discretion the better part of valour we're in the right place, for a change."

She smiled. "Yes, let's sit this one out and enjoy the show, Matilda has everything under control."

As people shouted, jumped about, did nothing useful, with some stealing unattended property, the dog tried to turn its head snapping at the cat, which made things worse as its ear dragged through Matilda's teeth.

With a howl and a vigorous shake, the dog finally escaped from the jaws of man's second-best friend and ran for its life.

As a modicum of calm descended upon the scene, people pitched in to help the cat family restore some order to the ideal sausage setting.

"Isn't that nice," said Mixie, "people can be so helpful in times of crisis, Dixie."

He looked at her, shook his head. "Look at that lot over there," he said, as the blare of sirens cut through the humid air. Following his pointing finger, she saw a group of young men fighting over some dispute involving touch rugby and other people arguing with the thieves of their stolen property.

"I just love the variety that humankind, bring to the tapestry of life, don't you, Dixie?" she said with a sad sort of smile.

He smiled, too, somewhat sadly. "There's no hope for them is there." Making his comment a statement not a question.

***

Later, as the pixies made their way homeward, one eavesdropping bird said to the other, "What Mixie suggested would work, wouldn't it?"

"Yes," said the other, "the elimination of Homo the Sap, would be the perfect answer for the complete recovery of the rest of us long suffering, flora and fauna."

***

The Synonym Tree

It was only two days later that the pixies happened to be out and about enjoying some well-earned rest and recreation after their recent adventures when a more sombre event took place.

An occurrence showing a side of Mixie seldom seen these days...

The mythological world, as with any other living space contains dark corners, where light chooses not to go, places where creatures dwell one wishes did not exist, but always have and always will.

However, rest assured, goodness, niceness and candy floss will always prevail, because, we all live in the reality of a fairy tale.

Then again, of course, one is not always sure, as life has an uncanny way of intruding on the best laid plans of, women, men and pixies.

There was not much happening at 2 a.m. with the southern hemisphere of this mortal coil waiting for the turmoil of yet another day to get underway. Author

The pixies had walked barefoot, with their jeans neatly rolled up, in the dew laden grass for an hour or more, when Mixie said, "Where are we?"

Dixie thought about her question for a moment, before saying, "We haven't been in this part of town before."

"No," she said, "and there's not a house in sight that I can see."

Half a moon looked at the pixies then decided not much was happening and went about its business; what the other half of the earth's companion was doing was anyone's guess.

Breaking the peaceful silence, Dixie mused more to himself than anyone else. "We have been moving in a north easterly direction, if that's any help."

Pixies have extraordinary night vision, similar to cats, and as Mixie looked about her, she said, pointing, "There's an interesting tree over there."

Approaching the tree that was aware of its visitors, Dixie said, "It looks as if it's leaning on its elbows."

And indeed, it did, with two humungous branches, which were more like trunks resting on the ground, as the rest of the arboreal giant wandered towards the starlit sky.

Climbing to the lower branches and quickly disappearing amongst the foliage, Mixie shouted back, "Not a native of this country, I would say."

As he joined her, Dixie took one of the glossy leaves in his hand, "What shape would you say that is?"

She looked, squinted, saying, "Um, a long oval, I think."

"Yeah," he mused, thoughtfully, "probably ended up here brought out by an early settler, way back."

She nodded her agreement. "Hmm, most likely, and there could have been habitation around here in those days."

"Do you think birds live in this tree?" he asked.

She thought about his far-reaching question, before saying, "Probably not, unless they are way up in the canopy, because this tree has easy access for humans."

He nodded. "Yeah, and we know what *Homo sapiens* are like."

Adjusting her position to lean back on a sturdy bough, she said, "I've been thinking."

Smiling, his eyes crinkling with mischief, he whispered, "How much trouble will we be in this time."

She gave him a kiss on the nose, something she had learned from observing human behaviour. "Probably not much."

Pulling a face, he said, "Huh, where's the fun in that?"

Smiling, her look encouraging, she said, "Do you have any favourite words, Dixie?"

He hesitated. "Um, I've never really thought about it, what would be an example?"

She looked at the non-interested moon, gathering her thoughts, before she said, "Well, I like the word, petulant."

"Hmm, why's that then?" he asked.

She shrugged. "Because I think it is a very descriptive word."

He frowned. "What of?"

"Well, um irritation or it could have another meaning, like animosity," she said.

"Yes," he agreed, "anything else?"

She hesitated. "Listen, what's that noise, is it a car?"

Looking in the direction from whence they came, he said, "It's a four-wheel drive by the sound of it."

Headlights came into view as a vehicle moved towards the pixies and stopped under the tree. The lights were turned off as the engine gave a shudder then stopped.

They heard a muffled scream.

Pixie eyes met in alarm, as a dark clad male driver got out and opened the rear door, the inner lights flooding the immediate area outlining two struggling figures.

A sobbing woman was pushed out followed by a man telling her to shut up.

"I don't like the look of this, Dixie," she whispered.

"No, and now I can see more clearly, I would say she is closer to sixteen than any other age," his voice took on an angry edge.

A few pixie seconds ticked by.

"I agree," she said, "and those two horrors are up to no good."

"Yeah, which way do you want to play this, Mixie?"

There were some murmurings from below, as she said, "You get onto the police with your mobile, give them the north easterly direction and the tree as a landmark."

"And?" he asked, already knowing the answer.

"And" – she sighed – "I will negotiate, but the situation could have gone too far already."

Shaking his head, Dixie said, "I thought we were finished with this goodie and baddie stuff from the old days."

Mixie drifted down to ground level, saying cheerfully, "Good morning, gentlemen, bit early for a picnic."

The bozo holding the girl gave a startled 'What the hell' as he pulled a flick knife out of his pocket and held it to his captive's neck.

With a flash of movement, Mixie moved behind the thug, giving him a rabbit punch to the base of his skull.

As he crumpled to the ground taking the girl with him, the knife dropped out of his hand.

Darting forward, bozo number two picked up the weapon and Mixie could see immediately he knew how to use it.

"Oh bugger, poor choice, sir, I wish you hadn't done that," she said, fixing him with her hypnotic mauve eyes.

The man with the knife, became bemused, not knowing why, as Mixie moved forward languidly and applied the pixie ear twist.

As the bozo fell to the ground with a scream, she said, "Whoops, sorry, I seem to have nicked your ear lobe in my enthusiasm."

With baddie number two squirming on the ground, Mixie added, "It's marvellous what they can do with plastic surgery these days, sir, cheer up, it could have been worse."

"All set," said Dixie, dropping to ground level, "do you need any help?"

She gave a tired sort of smile, as she said, "No, they're just pussy cats… Listen, that was quick, here come the boys and girls in blue," as two patrol cars sped towards them.

"Time, we made ourselves scarce," said Dixie, as they climbed to their evergreen sanctuary.

The patrol cars came to a halt, with headlights fixed on the scene before them.

"Jeez," said Gwen, getting out of the driving seat, "there's been more than a bit of kerfuffle here."

Her partner gave a 'here we go again' wag of his head. "I'll get some towels and gloves, can't be too careful."

The other two officers from the second car approached the girl, one saying, "What happened?"

His companion observing quickly. "Leave her, Steve, she's got that two thousand metre stare, she's in deep shock, I'll get a blanket for her, the ambulance will be here in a tick."

***

With the police and ambulance heading for civilisation, the pixies began to make their way homeward, as Dixie sensed the upheaval of that morning was still with her.

He squeezed her hand, she turned, gave him a smile. "Moving on," she said, like the battler of old, "how about the word, covetousness, Dixie?"

"What about it?"

"Well," she said, "don't you think it sounds like what it means, with other words ready to take its place?"

"Hmm, could be, such as?" he asked.

She gave him a sideways look and a smile. "For example, jealousy, gluttony, for a start."

He stopped suddenly, catching her off balance. "Do you know what I think?" he said.

"What?"

"I think we should name the tree we discovered, Synonym."

"What a fantastic idea, Dixie," she said, giving him a hug, that nearly squeezed the life out of him.

As dawn started to make up its mind, birds ruffled their feathers, the moon thought about its next move, he said, "You, okay?"

She looked at him, a weariness about her. "These days, stuff like that, does my head in a bit, but I'm okay now."

He nodded, put his arm around her, held her close, as they headed for home base, where Marmalade their cat would accept no excuses for not being fed on time.

***

Afterthought: This, so called fairy tale, illustrates the dark side of pixie folklore. No fairy dust or sparkles here, and as can be seen, Mixie can be unacceptably ruthless with baddies and bear the consequences.

The police interviews with the young woman and the alleged perpetrators were interesting.

(1) A move learned from her days working undercover with the, Pixie Regiment, in a previous life that left a few things buzzing around in her head. The tactics performed by Mixie should not be used at home, or anywhere.

***

The Art of Communication

Taking their time to recover from, what they now called the, 'Synonym' adventure, the pixies ventured once again into the realms of, observing humans in their day-to-day activities.

The pixies knew that in days gone by people thought good communication was a science and many attempts had been made to impose a regime for success.

However, out of the ether came the thought that, effective communication between flora fauna and or pixies is by and large based upon feelings, with a sprinkling of rational thinking for seasoning.

This theory is easily checked out the next time a decision is required. Author

***

So, where were the pixies?

The sky was grey, the sea reflecting the mood of whatever power made such things happen.

It was a windless day at a place called, Mission Bay, with the pixies sitting atop the tallest tree they could find, observing with interest, and as always, some uneasiness, what people were up to.

The beach was crowded with men, women and children, doing this that and the other, in a haphazard and in most cases harmless way.

On the golden sand plastic bags and cardboard boxes jostled for supremacy with the polymer winning the day, as sand filled containers lay inert unable to compete.

Pulling out her ultra-smart phone from the back pocket of her jeans, Mixie tapped and scrolled…

"What do you think of this, Dixie?" she said, proffering the device to her, one and only.

He looked, read aloud, "Good communication is understanding and being understood."

She sniffed in a knowledgeable way, saying, "How would you interpret that piece of mumbo jumbo jazz?"

Pursing his lips thoughtfully, and squinting his dazzling green eyes, he said, "I think the person that wrote that had the temerity to suggest an attempt be made to understand the other person or pixie before ramming one's own message down their throat."

Whilst this conversation was taking place, two birds settled on a branch next to the duo, pretending to mind their own business.

"Hmm, okay then, how reasonable do you think that adage is?" she asked.

"Totally off the page," he said, "surely the main point about communication is to ensure that the other person or pixie is mindful of what they are being told."

As they looked at each other, doubt in their eyes, Dixie added, thoughtfully, "On the other hand, when one thinks about it, I suppose there is some merit in knowing where the other person or pixie is coming from."

As Mixie was about to comment on the sagacity of Dixie's analysis, an almighty squealing, scrunching, expensive noise came from the direction of the road.

Hundreds of eyes immediately focused upon, Tamaki Drive, the road skirting, Mission Bay, where an expensive continental car had ploughed into the back of a bus that had stopped at the traffic lights.

"Interesting, the back of the car looks okay," said Dixie, as if he knew what he was talking about.

His companion nodded, thoughtfully saying, "Yes, however, I think the front will need some work."

As a man extricated himself from the badly bent car, he yelled to the bus driver, "You ******* moron, the lights had only just changed to red, you could have driven through."

"Oh look, Mixie, the bus driver is giving the man a signal with his finger," said Dixie.

Arching an eyebrow, she smiled, knowingly. "Yes, you could call it that."

In the meantime, before you could say, Jack Robinson (whoever that is), as far as the eye could see, both ways, was jammed packed with earth warming, throbbing, fuel guzzling machinery.

The only advantage being, some entity had switched on the sun, with resourceful people making the best of things by having a roadside picnic, because the rest of the day was stuffed.

In due course, two motorcycle cops arrived and brought further disorder to the scene by getting completely different versions of the free public entertainment event from the participants and rubberneckers.

The pixies smiled at each other, with Mixie saying, "There's a lot of communication taking place between the two drivers, Dixie."

"Yes," he said, "I wonder if they are trying to understand where the other is coming from?"

"Where there's a wheel there's a way," said one of the birds.

Mixie looked at the two avian creatures in astonishment. "This world is going crazy Dixie birds don't talk."

He looked at her, shaking his head, "Maybe not all the time, but they sure can communicate."

On their way home from the entertaining debacle and side show of, Mission Bay, the pixies came across an old man trying to cross a busy road.

"You would think, Dixie, there would be a pedestrian crossing on this stretch of road," she said.

"Yeah," he said, "but there are not many houses around here, it's mostly industrial, he could be lost."

"Well, there's only one way to find out, we'll go ask him," she said.

Approaching the old man, Mixie was the first to speak. "Hello, sir, it's like trying to cross a war zone out there."

The old man looked at her as if not at all surprised to be spoken to by a pixie. "Yes," he said, "it looks as if I took a wrong turn and ended up here."

"Where are you heading?" asked Dixie, taking a super smart mobile X3 from his pocket.

The old man took a piece of paper from his jacket, adjusted his glasses and read, "Morse Road, I'm visiting a friend that I haven't seen in years, and got off the bus back there." He pointed to his right.

Dixie did a bit of flick and poke, before saying, "Ah, yes, I see what must have happened, you turned left, from the bus, all you needed to do is turn to the right, Morse Road is back there." He pointed.

"Come on," said Mixie, cheerfully, "we'll show you the way."

"That's very kind of you, thanks," said the old man, "my name is Bob, and you must be a couple of pixies."

M & D stopped abruptly, astonished, with Mixie saying, "You, Bob, are among only a very few to have recognised us as pixies."

"Yes," said Dixie, "most people consider us to be, drones, androids, or some other weird device."

The old man smiled, he had an air of unusualness about him, an aura, as he said, "I had a relative, who died long ago, and her dining out story was about the time, many years in the past when she saw a pixie in a strawberry patch, and I was the only one that believed her."

Mixie, became still and quiet, traffic noise seemed to fade, her eyes widened, as she put her hand to her mouth, "Your relative, her name was, Gertrude, am I right, Bob?"

The old man's smile was slight, his eyes penetrating, as he said, "Yes."

And there, as they say, lies another story from long ago.

***

Note: The original source of the 'communication' adage has been lost in the mist of time…

For the record, bus drivers, do not proffer any part of their anatomy out of a window, door or any other aperture.

The naughty word used by the car driver ******* was, 'blasted', hmm.

***

An Interlude

The pixies were sitting at their dining room table listening to an interview on RNZ National, where a world-famous taxidermist was explaining the intricacies of preserving discarded banana skins…

"It's amazing how they do things like that, Dixie," she said.

He nodded. "Yeah, even a senior politician from overseas was fascinated by the process, it made him smile, apparently."

Frowning, Mixie said, "You mean guffaw, surely, a senior person like that doesn't waste time merely smiling, Dixie."

"No, of course not, it is a photo op after all, and he has more important things to do but he did say he liked the motto of the taxidermist," Dixie said, insightfully.

Mixie raised a quizzical eyebrow. "You mean their banner logo thingy, 'Stuff It'?"

"Well," explained, Dixie, "the senior politician said he liked the implied meaning, but he used another word, which caused a bit of a stir at the press conference."

As the pixies continued to listen to the incisive questioning of the interviewer the rain which had been a weak drizzle intensified and began to beat at the dining room window.

"We won't be going out in this weather, Dixie," she said, pulling her dressing gown even tighter around herself.

(Note: Pixies don't actually sleep, but they do rest, and wear the appropriate clothing at the time.)

"No," he said, "but, are you aware that today is Marmalade's flea stuff day, right? And have you noticed, we are a cat less household, she has strangely disappeared."

"She knows what is going to happen, the little toad," said Mixie.

Dixie smiled gently at the best pixie in the universe. "And you do know, that it is your turn to catch her, right, and administer the aforementioned flea stuff?"

Mixie slumped in her chair, panic stricken. "I've got a gut feeling it's not going to be a good day."

"Cheer up," he said, "you can tell me the story of how you met, Gertrude, after the flea fiasco."

She looked at her beloved through slit eyes. "You have to help me, because I assisted you last time by trapping her in a corner."

Sighing dramatically, he said, "Bugger, I thought you might have forgotten about that."

***

Later, that morning, she shook her head in despair. "How is it possible for a cat to get behind a stove that is hard up to the wall?"

"Yeah," he said, "surely there's only about a centimetre of room back there."

Everything was ready to go, even a butterfly net, which they weren't sure how that was going to work.

She looked at him, he looked back. "Do you think, we can shift the stove together, Dixie?"

Pixies are very strong, because of their origins (which is another story), so he said, "Probably, but she'll just dart away."

"We'll shut the doors and I'll use the sack technique, right?" she suggested.

"Hmm, okay," he agreed, "but we'll need gloves."

Long story made short; they wrestled the stove away from the wall.

They needn't have…

Halfway through puffing, panting and Dixie blaming Mixie, a dignified cat strolled out and sat in front of the stove.

Whereupon, Mixie, did the flea thing…

At which stage, Marmalade didn't speak to the pixies, for the rest of the day.

Or, at least, until she wanted her lunch and dinner after which all was forgiven, maybe.

***

With the lights on because of the darkness of the day and Marmalade having commandeered half the couch the pixies sat in their rocking chairs, that were called, Penny Rockers.

"So," said Dixie, "who was this mysterious, Gertrude, and what did you make of, Bob?"

She smiled at him, shaking her head, she said, "It was the 30th of February 1904."

Silence.

"Ah, yes." He too smiled. "You are using the mythological calendar."

"I am, indeed," she said, "that was the day I came into existence."

Silence.

"Which means," he said, "if my maths is correct, you are scheduled to go out of existence on the 30th of February 2053."

She sort of smiled, but it was sad. "Which means, Dixie, my due date to leave is before your one."

Silence.

Dixie took a breath, their eyes met and held. "It won't be the same, I'll be lost, but that is how the pixie world works," he said.

He got up, walked over to Mixie and wriggled in beside her.

"Now," she said, "about Gertrude."

"Yes" – he nodded – "tell me about, the mysterious Gertrude."

She thought, it's as clear now as it was back then… "I was in a strawberry patch and by the side of me those terrible old fashioned pixie clothes they used to dish out in those days."

He nodded, chuckled. "Yes, I remember, it was the same with me I could never keep the hat on."

They were very close he could see the tears in her eyes…

"Anyway" – she took a breath – "I got dressed quickly, and as I was watching this human family, they began to gather strawberries with the three kids stuffing the fruit down their throat."

"Needless to say," he said, "eventually they were ill."

"That's right, dreadfully, but after, just as I finished dressing, the smallest child caught sight of me, and yelled out that she had seen a little girl."

Mixie became silent, thinking back, all those years ago.

"Then what happened?" he asked.

She looked at him, pursed her lips. "Well, at the time I thought it best to make myself scarce, so I skipped behind a shed out of sight."

He nodded. "I think I know what's coming the rest of the family hadn't seen you."

She shook her head in despair. "Absolutely right, and her toad of a brother, I can remember as if it were yesterday, shouted out that Gertrude was lying."

Silence.

He put his arm around her.

"Yes, her father began to chastise her, the brother being the perfect child I came out from behind the shed and hopped on the roof, giving them a bow, with a flourish."

"They were gobsmacked, to say the least," he said.

She nodded. "Yes, but even then, I think it was only Gertrude that truly believed what she saw."

Silence.

Marmalade opened an eye, stretched, then decided it was not lunch time and reversed the procedure.

"What about, Bob?" he asked.

She gave him her thousand-watt smile. "Forget Bob," she murmured.

So, he did, it didn't take long to forget, Bob, under the circumstances.

A covey of raindrops discussed their latest deluge and decided to call it a day.

"It's stopped raining." He observed astutely.

"Hmm," she whispered back, "you could say that."

The cat raised her head, looked at the pixies, thinking those two can't even talk properly.

***

A thought for the day: When the past visits the present, be careful what you wish for.

***

Where Balmy Breezes Blow

Preface: Once upon a time, a scientist of a certain ilk or other, said, "We are all aliens of some sort or other."

He was laughed out of his university.

Author

***

The window ledge in the pixies lounge was wide and long enough to accommodate both a cat and Mixie at either end, prompting Dixie, to remark they both looked like odd bookends.

Marmalade ignored the remark, sitting Sphinx like thinking about her next meal, whilst Mixie peered through the net curtains at the softly illuminated street.

At one a.m. a street that appeared to sit comfortably marooned in the 1950s; a street that was sparsely occupied by people and pixies that kept their own business behind closed doors.

That on the street corner just along from the pixie abode sat a dairy that opened twenty-four seven, and sold, if required by a customer, one band aid, not a packet, one washer, not a box, and, more outrageously, one egg, not a carton.

Mixie, as usual, was looking for any sign of movement or things untoward, saying over her shoulder, "What are you reading, Dixie?"

He looked up, waving a magazine above his head. "Very interesting, very informative," he said, "this article could give a clue about pixie origins."

He immediately had the attention of his most favourite pixie in the cosmos.

She swung around giving Dixie full frontal attention, which was not without risk, considering her mauve eyes swept over him like a lint gathering brush.

"This better be good," she said, "I'm busy keeping an eye on the drones that are not supposed to be flying at night."

He made a 'who cares' face, waved the magazine again, saying, "It's quite complicated."

Smiling, she said nicely, "Put it in words Marmalade will understand."

The cat opened an eye, hearing her name, assuming her breakfast had been served early…it hadn't.

"Okay," said Dixie, "see what you make of this."

He then set out to explain in simple language that life on earth is, in part, alien.

Hmm, I should take notes…thought Marmalade then didn't.

"Are you two listening?" Dixie, admonished.

"Of course, we are," said Mixie, narrowing her eyes in false concentration.

"Okay," he said, "well, astrophysicists are saying half of the Milky Way comes from distant space driven by interstellar winds."

"Did you get that, Marmalade?" asked Mixie.

The cat twitched, thought no, did you?

"Also, you should know," continued Dixie, "there are scientist's that say we are made of star stuff, so how do you like them apples?"

"Now, that I understand," said Mixie, "I've been saying that for years."

It's the first time I've heard of it, thought Marmalade.

"Not only, but also," continued Dixie, getting all excited, "earth was produced in the heart of the stars before being flung into the universe by a giant explosion."

Marmalade thought for a moment. I never heard anything.

"Which means," explained Dixie, "we are made in part from matter created by explosions from distant galaxies."

"We must have missed that part, Marmalade," said Mixie.

*Hmm, I can't think of where I was at the time…*mused, the cat.

"And what's more," Dixie droned on, "science maintains we can all consider ourselves space travellers."

"I haven't noticed anything untoward over the past few years, have you, Marmalade?" asked Mixie.

The cat scratched behind an ear as she thought… *Only, at times, my dinner is not always as per our agreed schedule…*

"Are you two keeping up?" asked Dixie, suspiciously.

"How dare you," flared Mixie. "Of course we are… Is there going to be a test?" she asked, uneasily.

Ignoring Mixie's jibe, Dixie said, "The same scientists maintain that much of the Milky Way matter was in other galaxies before it was kicked out by powerful galactic winds, travelling across space and eventually found a new home in our spot of the Cosmos."

Nodding wisely, Mixie intoned, "I think I will rest more easily knowing all that, what say you, Marmalade?"

The cat stopped taking notes that she hadn't started.

Just as Dixie was about to continue with his diatribe, the doorbell rang.

Mixie straightened from her slumped position, Dixie dropped his magazine and Marmalade opened both eyes.

Turning abruptly to look out the window Mixie's jaw dropped as there under the front door light which had automatically turned on, was that famous Chinese pixie, Trixie.

"It's Trixie!" she whooped.

And indeed, it was, the pixie that was a computer whizz kid and all things electronic.

Trixie, the behind-the-scenes operator in an obscure government department that tracked and brought to justice, Triads and kidnappers of rich people's children, reaping huge rewards from grateful parents.

The pixie with icy blue eyes and air of invincibility about her.

A pixie that always dressed immaculately and was presently wearing a silk lemon Mandarin collar trouser suit, with shoes that matched her eyes she was a force to be reckoned with. As the duo reached the front door, they were in time to see the Embassy limo pull away and disappear into the darkness.

While all this was happening, Marmalade considered the prospect of three pixies in the one house and reached the conclusion that very little justice prevailed for the cats of this world.

As all three pixies kissed air and hugged (behaviour copied from humans), Dixie said, "You could have let yourself in you, know the numbers."

Trixie smiled. "That wouldn't have been proper," she said, in perfect English.

"Why didn't you let us know you were coming?" said M & D in unison.

"That would have spoilt the surprise, besides, certain things happened and I had to get my A into G fast, I'm on a mission, needless to say," said Trixie, as she put her chamois leather briefcase on the hall table.

A glance passed between M & D, with Mixie saying, "Uh oh, here we go again."

Trixie gave her pixie comrades a beneficent smile. "You both love it, don't deny a thing."

Everyone laughed, accept Marmalade.

"Come on bring your stuff into the lounge and give us the gory details," said Dixie.

Before they settled down, Trixie gave Marmalade a smooth and talked to her in Cantonese and Mandarin which the cat understood perfectly, being multi-lingual.

Somewhat mollified the feline withheld her judgment, until you know what hit the fan, later.

"So, what's the deal?" asked Mixie.

"Well, very long story short," said Trixie, "we are on the trail of a world-wide web of money laundering and drugs, part of which is in this country."

She opened her briefcase and took out a white envelope and handed to Mixie, saying, "Both of you have a look at that, what is it?"

Mixie took the envelope, held it up to the light, Dixie leaned in closer, he took it, flipped it open, smelt it…

"Well?" said Trixie.

"That is a good quality envelope," said Dixie.

"Yes," agreed Mixie, "one of those envelopes, that usually has a nine-dollar birthday card in it and is never on special."

"Hmm," said Trixie, "what if I told you that envelope is almost one hundred percent cocaine once it's been reconstituted."

Silence.

Before the pixies could react, Trixie fumbled in her brief case and withdrew a ball of white string, held it up saying, "Same thing."

Without further ado, Mixie said, "What do you want from us?"

"The use of your nicely tucked away secret computer office, simple… Well, sort of," said Trixie, with a shrug.

Dixie looked at Mixie, and said, "It's all in the shrug, isn't?"

Shaking her head, but smiling, Mixie said, "That shrug hides a thousand Chinese puzzles."

"I knew you would love it," said Trixie, with a mischievous smile.

Marmalade, absorbing all of this information, thought humans haven't got a chance…

Dixie did a knowledgeable sniff. "Why our computer set up, Trixie, it's pretty humble."

The computer maestro smiled. "Not by the time I've finished with it; all that old stuff is going, I will be installing equipment that hasn't been invented yet, sort of." She shrugged.

"There's that shrug again, Dixie," said his partner in crime, "she wants our place for other reasons, I'm thinking."

Trixie nodded. "Yes, of course, I've done my homework, you two are no slackers when it comes to computers, and this place is so secluded even the FBI are unaware it, and with a dairy that will sell one egg at a time, it's off the map, perfect!"

"So, when can we expect all this high-tech equipment?" asked Dixie.

Another smile from Trixie. "Listen," she said, "is, that a truck pulling up at your front gate?"

The time was 2.30 a.m.

"Where did you manage to get a delivery at this time in the morning?" asked Dixie.

Those blue eyes shimmered. "The Embassy."

"I give in," said the only male pixie in the vicinity.

It pays to thought Marmalade when you're dealing with pixies.

***

Now cometh implementation of the plan, ah yes, the plan.

Meet Broderick and Bobby the wife and husband van team.

Dixie got a, 'shut up' look from Mixie when he asked which was which.

Stack new stuff in lounge.

Remove old stuff and place in van.

Van returns to Embassy.

Unpack new stuff.

Stack packaging in hallway for removal later.

Do not try to read instructions because they will be in Chinese, this suggestion by Trixie even made Marmalade laugh.

Install new stuff, which became an average size miracle.

Now, this is when reality takes over.

Plans of mice, men and women often go astray (someone once said that)

Plans of pixies always go awry but are forever entertaining.

For example, Mixie became lost in the mountain of generated polystyrene and continued yelling loudly in 'marine' language until found and released.

Dixie explained to Trixie that 'marine' language contained many references to human body parts.

Marmalade became entrapped within a piece of computer equipment, which had to be completely disassembled to release her.

The cut finger that Dixie sustained required copious amounts of sympathy and one band aid purchased from the corner dairy.

Apart from all the above everything went smoothly.

Throughout all the mayhem and misadventure Trixie remained cool, calm and collected performing the job of supervision with aplomb and not a hair out of place.

And, as Trixie explained, the objective was to completely disrupt the plans and distribution of baddie goods and services.

Ironically, because baddie people had kept up with and ran their business using modern technology it also led to their destruction.

However, as Trixie also informed the duo, as one part of the baddie scenario is closed down so another pops up to pursue their nefarious goals.

How come asked M & D? Because the baddies create a public demand for their products, explained Trixie, and people fall for their services every time.

How sad is that thought, Marmalade.

Some days later, with Marmalade spread across both their laps, a CD of small group jazz playing softly in the background, lights down low, Mixie said, softly, "I wish we could really find out about our origins, Dixie."

The pixies held hands in a world where they were aliens, but not baddies, hmm.

***

More of the Same Thing (R13 rating)

Preface: When life repeats itself what does that mean? It means that life repeats itself because we are all creatures of habit, especially if what we do brings pleasure. But you already knew that.

Then again, what about the not so good things that are repeated?

"What do you think of that?" asked Dixie.

***

At three a.m., the pixies and Marmalade were ten minutes from home walking barefoot in the dew laden grass, a favourite pastime for Mixie and Dixie; for the cat, not so much, wet fur not being her ideal state, but she liked being with her companions.

The second most favourite hobby for the duo was climbing trees, all the better to view human activity, in relative safety.

Marmalade also found climbing trees an enjoyable experience, and unlike many other cats had learned to back down, then turn when a metre or so from the ground and spring off.

Whereas other cats climbed trees with great enthusiasm only to be struck with fear when facing the task of returning earthwards headfirst.

This is why the fire service was invented, to rescue cats…

Meanwhile, birds farted gently and snuggled closer.

As they walked there came a gentle buzzing sound, with Dixie saying, "That's your mobile."

His offsider fished in her back pocket extracting the device and activating its wizardry. "It's, Trixie!" she exclaimed.

"Where are you?" asked, Trixie.

Mixie smiled at her companions, before saying, "We are happily in a paddock about ten minutes from home, why, where are you?"

"Mexico," was the reply.

Taking a deep breath and now speaking with a touch of, what the heck, Mixie said, "Where in, Mexico?"

"We are in a cupboard," murmured the rich Chinese pixie.

Dixie looked at Mixie, who looked back, while Marmalade looked at them both.

Dixie spoke first, "When you say we, the other being?"

"The other being, Vixie," explained the cupboard dweller.

"What? We thought Vixie was in Cornwall," said Mixie.

"Hmm, yes, well, I needed some help and didn't want to impose on your good selves again so early in the piece," explained Trixie.

There was, muffled murmurings from Mexico…

"How are you, Vixie, long time no see," said M & D in unison.

"Humph!" came from Vixie, aptly named after the vixen for her forceful personality.

"She's broken her wrist," said Trixie, with a sigh.

M & D's eyes met, both shaking their head, with Mixie asking, "How did that happen?" Sort of knowing, anyway.

There came more murmurings, from Mexico, with Trixie saying, "She hit a baddie a smidgen too hard."

"A smidgen," said Mixie, knowing otherwise.

Another sigh came from, Trixie, "Well, a couple of smidgens, I suppose."

*You better start explaining yourself, Trixie...*thought Marmalade.

"You better start explaining yourself, Trixie," said Mixie.

"Yeah, well." And so she did.

A Mexican drug cartel deep into supplying the demand from an ever-clamouring public.

A high-tech business now, not reliant on mules with brim full condoms.

Not reliant on suitcases crammed with cash.

Now business on the internet and shipping containers full of drugs masquerading as innocuous stuff.

With Trixie and other agencies using technology to hoist baddies on their own petard.

However, in the case of the Mexico junket, local low-tech equipment wasn't up to scratch.

"So," said Trixie, "Vixie and I need the services of your good selves, before the baddies find us in this cupboard."

"We won't ask how come you are in a cupboard," said Mixie, kindly, "as long as you are safe."

"Thank you for that, it is a tad embarrassing," murmured Trixie.

"How can we be of help?" asked Dixie, automatically turning for home.

Mutterings from Mexico, then from Trixie. "We need you to use the same programme we used before, with a few adjustments and me giving you the local crap to make it work this end."

"Then the baddies will be so bewitched, buggered and bewildered, we'll make our escape," said the pixie nursing a sore wrist. There was an underlying edge to her voice.

The phone went dead as if underlining Vixie's sentiments.

Smiling, Mixie said, "What I've always liked about Vixie is the succinct way she can sum up a situation."

As they made their way homeward post haste, Dixie remarked, thoughtfully, "Yes, she's always had a way with words."

That has been my impression, thought Marmalade, disliking her wet paws intensely.

***

That evening, with the news that yet another Mexican drug cartel had had their algorithm's truncated M & D relaxed, watching their favourite videos.

"What one shall we have next?" asked Mixie.

Tap dancing his way across the lounge, Dixie said, "I like that musical one," then did a nifty step or two much to the amusement of his other half. And so, on went, a great old musical with M & D dancing up a storm mimicking another era dancers to perfection, plus a few of their own innovations.

Exhausted, Marmalade watched from the safety of the window ledge, until finally the pixies fell on the couch gasping and clapping.

Recovering fast, Dixie sat up saying, "Okay, one for the road."

"What's it going to be?" she asked.

He looked at her, smiled. "Space Monster 13, you know how much you like the ending."

She thought for a moment. "Yes, right, that's where that woman has quad aliens out of her stomach, I like the part where they staple her up after."

"Yes," he said, "messy, but brilliant."

That was a movie Marmalade couldn't bear to watch, so she retired to Mixie's room for a well-earned rest.

Afterthought: The only thing left to say is, nothing changes, because right now the illicit drug business is still alive and kicking…

Why is that do you think?

Signed: Mixie, Dixie, Trixie, Vixie and Marmalade

***

A Barnum and Bailey World

Preface: In the quasi world of pixies, anything is possible.

They sat at opposite ends of the table in a public park under a tree eating their lunch.

The woman biting into her roll and chewing slowly, thinking, will the straw in my milkshake end up in the stomach of an animal or a fish.

Meanwhile, the man ingesting his sandwich hungrily was chewing with his mouth open, which is not an easy thing to do.

Swallowing her well masticated, delicate portion of egg, cheese and tomato, the woman said, to no one in particular… "What do you think the difference is between belief and faith?"

The man belched and still chewing a mouthful of his double bacon and triple egg sandwich, mumbled, whilst spitting food on the table. "Belief, madam, is faith in something that cannot be proven."

As the man pronounced his deep-thinking homily birds waited patiently for their share of his lunch.

Taking a deep breath, the woman narrow eyed the man, saying, haughtily, "Interesting, I've always thought of faith as belief in something that cannot be proven."

A distant crunching sound signalled yet another road accident whilst the rustle of leaves and twittering of hungry birds brought an eventual tranquil silence over the scene; the couple lost in their own thoughts.

Eventually, the woman and man both stood and without further ado went their separate ways.

She, taking her debris with her, whilst he, leaving his mess behind him, claiming inwardly that he was creating employment for the less fortunate of this world.

As the woman walked back to her office, she threw her rubbish at an overflowing garbage bin and was bang on target, smiling with some pride.

However, as she continued work-ward she kept thinking of the straw and its small but significant contribution to a global disaster.

The broken camel's back loomed in front of her, metaphorically speaking.

Retracing her steps quickly, the woman was in time to see a bird retrieve the straw for nesting purposes.

She smiled humbly this was a sign of faith, she thought.

Meanwhile, as the man strolled casually towards his six-cylinder behemoth he regretted indulging in the refluxing greasy sandwich.

But, at the same time was proud to have contributed to a job opportunity for the deserving poor.

As his machine roared into life, he told himself…it is people like me that will save this planet…a sign of belief, he thought. Author

***

The pixies gathered on the sundeck of M & D's villa.

Marmalade sitting on the edge of the roof gazed down upon the pixie ensemble, thinking… *What have I done to deserve this?*

What Marmalade meant by the word 'this' was a house full of pixies. Noisy, feisty, never still creatures, always up to some mischief.

The successful debacle of Mexico behind them, Trixie and Vixie had taken a short holiday in a place called, Guanabara Bay, and were now fully recovered ready to impose their expertise on any situation containing baddies.

At that very moment, the four pixies were sitting at a table their laptops and smart phones in front of them, strangely, in this day and age, each also had, by their side, a pencil and writing pad, hmm.

What does that tell us?

Anyway, moving on, Vixie was about to report on her visit to, Cornwell, as part of her research into, pixie-mania.

"We need the sun brolly up," said Trixie, very aware of safeguarding her skin from nuclear magnetic resonance.

M & D brought forth the brolly, one of those flash models that had a wind-up thingy to raise and lower it.

Now looking down at a brolly and no pixies, Marmalade decided to abandon the roof, and instead, sit under the table, where she could hear everything that was said.

Peering beneath the table, Vixie growled. "Do we have to have the cat under our feet?"

"Yes!" said Mixie adamantly. "She's part of the family."

"Humph!" was Vixie's opinion of that claim.

Dixie looked at the three other pixies, and said calmly, with a smile, "Shall we get on with it, before Cornwell disappears off the map."

Three pairs of female pixie eyes settled him…

"When you're ready," he said.

Marmalade stretched out, with Mixie and Dixie burying their feet in her fur. "Hmm," she purred.

Looking at the three other pixies and under the table, Vixie said, with a long-suffering sigh, "My research, of course, was interrupted by a sojourn to little old Mexico, so the report on pixie-mania will be somewhat disjointed."

The three other pixies and a cat waited with bated breath.

A helicopter thudded by so all communication was temporarily suspended for the duration.

Eventually, Vixie said, with great patience, "We already know heaps of the stuff I discovered, but it was good to have it confirmed."

The same helicopter re-thudded once again, with Vixie showing even greater patience at the additional interruption. "Will I shoot it out of the sky?" she asked, in a reasonable tone and lop-sided grin.

"Not today," said Trixie, "what is it we already know?"

"Well," continued Vixie, as the whirly bird disappeared towards the sun, "we happen to live in a quasi-world right now, well sort of, especially for some human beings."

Dixie sniffed intelligently. "You had better explain the word, quasi to Marmalade, Vixie," he said with a smile of encouragement.

The researcher looked under the table as the cat raised her head, with half open eyes. "Are you listening?" asked Vixie. The cat fully opened her eyes. Still looking under the table, Vixie said, "A, quasi world, is almost but not really, did you get that?" Marmalade blinked. Resurfacing, Vixie murmured, to herself, "I don't think she got that."

"Yeah." Nodding wisely, Dixie thought out loud. "You may have to rephrase, or something."

There was silence for a moment or three, bees foraged, a butterfly fluttered, birds exchanged gossip.

Finally, Vixie said, thoughtfully, "Something that resembles but is not actually the real thing."

She looked under the table, where a light bulb had flashed above Marmalade's head, as she thought... *You mean like some of my relatives that look like cats smell like cats, but are not real cats, because they are, woofters...*

Smiling, Vixie said, "I think she's got it."

"So, this Barnum and Bailey world we are living in right now, is, simply put, some people can imagine real pixies, others not so much." Dixie did that sniff of his and looked around the group.

"Couldn't have summed it up better myself," said Vixie, as they all looked under the table where Marmalade had fallen asleep through sheer boredom...

"How about a short break, we should have a look around the garden and annoy all the critters or something," suggested Trixie.

Removing her feet from Marmalade's furry tummy, Mixie said, "Yes, good idea, my toes have got pins and needles."

Dixie gave a wink to Mixie, and looking at their guests, said, "You two can help us get the washing in."

So that's what they did, with Trixie saying, "This is a real novelty for me."

After gathering in the bits and pieces, they sat beneath an out of control, Jacaranda tree, with Mixie pointing out, several bird's nests.

"I don't see any birds," said Vixie.

Dixie shook his head in mild despair. "Vixie, the birds are in the privacy of their own nest, or out and about getting something to eat."

"Oh," she said, "that bowl of water by the hedge, what is that for, Marmalade?"

Mixie laughed. "No way, her water has to be pristine, that is for the hedgehogs."

There was a smidgen of excitement from, Vixie. "I want to see the hedgehogs please."

"Hedgehogs do not come forth on command for our entertainment," said Mixie.

"You'll have to be here late evening, when it's almost dark, that's when our prickly friends venture out for a drink," said Dixie.

"Okay," Vixie clapped her hands, "do hedgehogs believe in pixies?"

"Absolutely," said Dixie, "they are part of our B and B world."

As they made their way back to the sundeck, Vixie said, "During my ferreting around, I came across some interesting information about, Barnum and Bailey, and how people can be easily fooled."

"You must tell us about that," said Trixie, the undercover agent.

As they settled around the table once again, the only member of the group missing was, Marmalade.

"Yes," said Mixie, "I would say she is out front chasing off dogs that try to pee against our front gate."

"I would like to see that," said Vixie.

So, they all trooped through the house to look out the lounge window.

Sure enough, Marmalade was hiding behind a low hedge that ran across the front of the property.

After several minutes, Vixie grumbled, "There's nothing happening."

"This is not a show that opens and closes on time," Dixie informed her, "wait on, wait on, here comes a person with his Pit Bull terrier, let's see what happens."

As the canine person was passing the pixies place, the dog on a leash, lunged for the gate.

Outshot Marmalade, leapt over the hedge and buried a claw in the dog's nostril.

The dog let out a blood curdling howl as the canine person pulled on the leash and the cat tugged at the soft flesh, it was not a pretty sight.

Finally releasing the dog, Marmalade gave her best hissing fit, puffing up her fur to look twice her normal size.

The canine lover gathered up his precious dog and ran for both their lives.

Vixie was beside herself (her favourite position) clapping and cheering, shouting, "This is the best entertainment I've seen in years; I now love your cat to bits."

The other three pixies were rocking with laughter, as Trixie finally said, "Come on you lot, we have work to do."

As the pixies resettled, Trixie said, "Before we get into more pixie stuff, tell us about this, Barnum and Bailey thingy, Vixie."

"Yes," she said, "I came across it by chance, it was interesting, way back in the late eighteen hundred early nineteen hundred, of course."

"Wow, even before your time, Mixie," said her most favourite pixie, with a smile.

She gave him a 'look', which said… I'll get you later, on my terms…

"Anyway," continued Vixie, "early in the piece B & B had these freak shows, way before the, 'Greatest Show on Earth', circus thingy."

"Hmm, they wouldn't be allowed to use the word freak, these days," said Trixie.

Mixie nodded her agreement. "No, indeed, that would be totally politically incorrect."

"So, what were these freakish thingies?" asked Dixie, who, unlike today's general public wanted to know about such things.

"Um," Vixie thought for a moment, "well, there was, The Bearded Lady, and, The Fattest Man, in the world, and, um, The Rubber Man, plus others."

"What did the Rubber Man do?" asked Dixie.

"Tied himself in knots, quite creepy," she said.

"Anything else?" asked, Mixie.

"Yes," said Vixie, with a laugh, "there was the man that lived in a glass box with a hundred rats."

Trixie threw up her hands in disgust. "Get to the point about fooling people."

Nodding, Vixie said, "Yes, B and B were clever buggers, in the early days they had these closed off booths, usually in a big hall or marquee; and charged people before they entered each booth."

"That sounds fair," said Dixie.

"Yes," agreed Vixie, "only problem was people were hanging around too long and not moving through."

Smiling, Trixie said, "Yes, turnover of people, keep the public moving, so what did they do?"

Vixie tapped the side of her nose. "They gave something away for free that would keep the crowd moving."

A cheer went up as Marmalade returned, then applause as she settled under the table on M & D's feet.

"So, what happened," Dixie asked.

"Well," said Vixie, "there was usually a door at the back of the hall or marquee, so they put up a large notice with an arrow pointing to the door, saying, 'Free Egress'."

Smiling, Trixie clapped her hands. "And the crowds moved more quickly in order to get a look at the, free egress."

"Brilliant," said Mixie, "and what they got was indeed the egress that is, the way-out door."

"Hmm, good stuff," said Dixie, "probably wouldn't work these days, but way back then, yeah."

The pixies relaxed, the day softened, a bee settled on the table, looked at the pixies for a brief moment then was gone.

Trixie said, "Where were we?"

"We are supposed to be reviewing all the fantastic research that Vixie worked her butt off for," said Dixie.

Under the table Marmalade thought… *They couldn't organise a piss up in a brewery…*

"That's right," said Mixie, "what else have you got for us, Vixie?"

"Ah yes," said the researcher, letting out a puff of air, "it's a bit of a mixed bag and needs further work" – raising her eyebrows – "without interruption."

Trixie smiled, patted Vixie's hand saying, "Give it your best shot, sweetheart."

"Well," she said with a rush, "I'll give you a summary of the boring old stuff, to set the scene." And counted off on her fingers…

"All pixies are the same height,

All pixies are the same weight,

All pixies have an extraordinary sense of hearing and smell,

All pixies are very strong,

All pixies have distinctive eyes,

All pixies must avoid swimming pool water it's the chemicals apparently, because we take all our nourishment through our skin, by rainwater, sun and air."

Vixie laughed (which was unusual). "Got you with that last one, but it's true."

M & D's eyes met; they had got rid of an above ground swimming pool some time ago because the chemical content had started to attack their skin.

"Well, that is worth knowing and important," said Trixie, "anything else?"

Vixie took a deep breath. "I got the impression that it is widely accepted pixies first came to human notice in, Cornwell, England. Also they lived in the high moorland of Devon. But I question that because there are pixies all over the world, but under different names."

"Yes," said Trixie, with a beaming smile, "me for example."

"Anything else?" asked Mixie.

Vixie peered at her laptop. "Heaps and heaps of fine detail."

"Give us the guts of it," suggested Dixie.

Looking and fiddling, Vixie said, "This is quite interesting, as we know pixies are wingless, but can never-the-less fly through the air over short distances, which is very handy in tricky circumstances."

"Hmm, any clue as to how we do that?" asked Mixie.

"Yes," continued Vixie, "it's still under review, but it is thought the shape and largish size of our ears are apparently aerodynamically suited to give us lift off, and we instinctively flit here and there, especially when under some form of pressure."

"Wow, that is new information," said Trixie, "I've always suspected there was a logical explanation."

Again, the eyes of M & D met, they had come across such detail in the past.

"What else have you got?" asked Dixie. "This is getting interesting."

"Heaps, but I'll keep it short," said Vixie, "I don't want to miss the hedgehogs."

Under the table, Marmalade opened her eyes winced, remembering her first hedgehog encounter, resulting in a sore nose and paws, thinking… *If I had to chase hedgehogs from our front gate, it would be floating in pee for all I care…*

"There is still plenty of time for hedgehog spotting, Vixie," said Dixie.

"Yes, come on," encouraged Mixie, "confirming certain details has been enlightening stuff, so far."

Vixie looked at the screen, fiddled and faddled, saying, "Apparently, pixies back in the day showered blessings on local people. They were mostly joyful creatures, and usually up to some mischief or other…"

Under the table, Marmalade uttered a small groan.

"I think the cat agrees with that last part," said Trixie, as M & D laughed, but the researcher didn't.

"Here's a part I like," said Vixie, "pixies often led humans astray, but were never malevolent in fact they went out of their way to help local citizens."

The other three pixies smiled and clapped.

"That sounds more like us," said Dixie.

"Yeah, well," shrugged Vixie, "that's about it for now I need more time, at this stage."

"How much time?" Trixie asked. "Just in case something comes up."

The information gatherer thought for a moment as the late afternoon meandered on at its own pace. "Couple of weeks," she said, "providing I'm not interrupted."

Then she sat bolt upright staring at the screen.

"What is it?" said M & D in unison.

Vixie pointed at her laptop. "Something I've overlooked about the origins of everything in our galaxy."

Mixie and Dixie were suddenly knocked out of the torpidity orbit they were in and became super interested.

"Do tell do tell," said Mixie excitedly, "this is the most important part of all."

"Yes," Dixie backed up his partner, "there's a hedgehog in it for you if it's good stuff."

"Hmm," said Vixie, "there is information, but you may be a smidgen disappointed."

The three other pixies and Marmalade waited with bated breath, which is not easy to do.

"The problem has been," said Vixie, checking to see if Marmalade was listening, she wasn't, "has been sorting out fantasy from reality."

"Yeah," said Dixie, with a shake of his head, "human beings are continually having that problem."

"Anyway," continued, Vixie, "I came across a six-hundred-page thesis, which we won't dwell on today."

Waking momentarily, Marmalade thought... *Who in the cosmos do we have to thank for that...?*

"Go on," said Dixie, "give us the truncated version."

"Okay," agreed Vixie, "the theories and conclusions were by some astrophysicist, several years ago at a university."

Dixie stood suddenly, interrupting the oracle, tipping Marmalade onto the sundeck, where she sat bemused, which is very easy for a cat to do.

"Just a minute!" said Dixie, "I've read somewhere about that," looking at Mixie with a frown, for confirmation.

She frowned back...

Marmalade frowned in sympathy, but not in knowing.

Vixie arched an eyebrow. "Was it the scientists who said, each one of us, including pixies is made from matter created when suns exploded in distant galaxies?"

This time, Mixie nodded. "Yes, I remember it now Dixie had set out to bore us to death."

He almost succeeded... Thought the cat...

"Continuing," said Vixie, "the other bit of info I've gleaned so far is, trillions of years ago there was more than one universe."

She stopped and smiled at her captive audience.

"Really," said Trixie, looking into the half distance with a dazed expression, "what happened?"

"I'll spare you the details," Vixie, smiled kindly, "the theory being worked on right now is six universes collided with each other, edgewise, and…"

"Stop, stop, stop." A cry rent the air from three pixies in unison.

Whilst under the table, Marmalade thought, *What a shame, it was just getting to the interesting part.*

"What's the problem?" asked Vixie.

"Information overload," said Dixie, with a gasp of despair.

As Trixie and Mixie exchanged a glance, Mixie said, "All this info is not going to tell us about our specific origins, is it?"

With a sigh, Vixie murmured, "No, because it appears the basic building blocks of everything and everyone could have originated from out there. somewhere."

She waved towards the stars.

"Hmm," said Dixie.

"Hmm," said Mixie.

"Hmm," said Trixie.

*I don't really care anymore…*thought Marmalade.

"Can I see the hedgehogs now please?" asked Vixie quietly and politely.

Dusk was gathering because it had nothing better to do.

Birds snuggled in their nests.

Countless stars dreamt of super nova.

"I think Vixie has earned her way onto the hedgehog calendar," said Dixie, looking at M & T.

The two pixies nodded their agreement.

And so, the pixies wandered into the twilight world of a mammal that has more sense than the spines on its back.

***

Addendum: To: Mixie, Dixie, Trixie and Marmalade
From: Vixie

Whilst exploring a dusty obscure library in, Truro, I came across a thousand-page document which I sent to you as an attachment.

I haven't heard anything back from you guys as yet…

There are several items of interest to which I draw your attention relevant to my research into pixie-mania.

Apparently, by chance, many years ago a group of, bird watchers which is a similar occupation to, drying paint researchers, discovered the coming into this world of a pixie.

I knew immediately that you would be interested…

Put briefly and simply we came about via a chrysalis process, a form of metamorphosis, which no doubt is part of the 'star dust' enigma we discussed some time ago, via Skype (when Marmalade fell off your, baby grand piano sound asleep).

I'm sure you remember the occasion.

Also, your theory, Dixie, that our initial clothing was tailored by elves is bang on target.

I am presently in the process of summarising the thousand-page tome into a more readable format i.e., a digest of 499 pages.

I look forward to discussing my findings with you early next month.

Trixie, as we speak is on some weird boring assignment involving a place called, Kilimanjaro.

Oh yes, the other day I shot down a drone, they are noisy little bastards, most annoying.

Give my regards to the hedgehogs.
Vixie

***

Give It Your Best Shot

Preface: Justice is a convoluted process because when it appears not to have worked, it hasn't.

Author

***

There were four pixies, a cat and several birds sitting in a tree of unknown genus overlooking a playing field where games of cricket were taking place.

Marmalade had been threatened with a fate worse than death if she even thought about a bird lunch.

At which stage the cat thought… *How did Mixie know what I was thinking?*

It was then that Mixie said, "I know exactly what you are thinking, Marmalade."

I give up thought the cat…that is uncanny and eerie…

Looking at the playing area, what was there to see?

It was large, with three games taking place at the same time.

Weather wise the day was a balmy 27C with a haze of grey cloud causing some glare for the batsmen.

Breaking the silence, Dixie said, "Tell us about this drone thingy you shot out of the sky, Vixie." (Please see special postscript in due course regarding Vixie's behaviour.)

Before the sharpshooter could get underway, Trixie said, "Give us the condensed version, please, not chapter and verse."

I wonder how boring this is, going to be? Marmalade thought.

Similar thinking went through the bird's brains as they waited for the lunch break, with the usual good pickings left underfoot by the cricket enthusiasts.

Shaking her head in frustration, Vixie said, "You lot don't deserve a good yarn, I've a good mind to reduce the story to less than a thousand words."

There was a collective sigh of resignation with all thinking... *We haven't anything better to do.*

"What weapon did you use?" asked Dixie.

"Yeah, good point," said Vixie, "I'm not really sure, it was called a slug gun, which I borrowed."

"Yes, I know," said Dixie, "the ammunition is those little lead slugs, they are not very lethal."

"Tell me about it," grumbled Vixie, "and only one shot before a reload."

Mixie coughed in a superior way, saying, "So, you didn't have your semi-automatic with you."

"Tell me about it," Vixie shook her head, "they won't let them through customs these days, not even in the diplomatic bag."

Raising an eyebrow, Trixie said, "I hate to ask this, but what led up to the fateful day?"

Leaning back against the trunk of the tree to gain a more comfortable position, much to everyone's horror the signs were ominous for a long haul, from Vixie the gun toting pixie.

The storyteller narrowed her eyes, looking around the group, she took a deep breath. "There was this kid about twelve, thirteen and he used a drone to spy on the neighbourhood."

"Uh oh," said Dixie, "a Peeping Tom."

"Yes, and to cut a long story short (a sigh went around the group), he was caught and ended up in some juvenile court where he was awarded community service and counselling."

Vixie finished her explanation, looked at the pixies, smiling, waiting...

"You mean sentenced, surely," said Mixie.

Another self-satisfied evil grin from, Vixie.

"All right," said Dixie, "I'll fall for it, what was his community service?"

"Teaching other kids how to use drones properly," said Vixie, with a look of despair and disbelief.

There was a long silence, before Mixie plucked up the courage to ask, "What happened next?"

"I'm glad you asked," said Vixie, "the young fellow not only trained other children to fly the nasty drones, he also continued his spying," she paused ominously, "including my room!"

There was a collective intake of breath the youth had committed the ultimate crime, intrusion upon a pixie and her privacy.

They all waited, gobsmacked, even the birds stopped chattering.

Marmalade thought… *I think the next bit of this story is going to disturb me…*

The slight smile on Vixie's lips didn't reach her eyes, her demeanour was remote.

Marmalade looked at the cricket trying to concentrate on the game but to no avail.

The mantle of the cold assassin settled over and around Vixie, as she said quietly, "I borrowed the slug gun thingy and thought about what best to do next."

Everyone paused, and even the cricketers went to lunch.

Eventually, Vixie said, "I thought, how best to get this young man's attention, how best for him to learn to be a good fellow?"

All waited, eager now to hear Vixie's version of, community service, wondering when this long-winded story was going to end.

"Sure enough," said Vixie, "the dear little chap was once again given another warning and increased community service, plus additional equipment to train other wayward children…"

The world as we know it appeared to stop spinning after this announcement from the sniper:

The normal noises and events of the day seemed to hang in the balance…

There were no crashes on the motorway…

The local tinny house ran out of product…

The corner dairy did not suffer its daily smash and grab…

The dairy owner having to delete the date on his insurance claim.

"And so," said Vixie, simply, with great patience, "the next time a drone came near my window, I shot it out of the sky."

She waited, looked around the group, defiant, they knew there was more to come.

"No one came near me to cart me off to prison," Vixie continued, "and the very next day, another drone with our little lad at the controls came buzzing around the neighbourhood, and so I shot that one out of the sky, as well, and from then on there were no more, until…"

Silence, with everyone present, except Marmalade, appalled at Vixie's bad behaviour.

The vixen smiled. "Then a few days later, I received a 'Thank You' card from the whole neighbourhood."

The world started to spin again:

The cricketers trundled onto the field…

The smashes on the motorway commenced once again with increased enthusiasm…

The dairy owners braced themselves for business as usual.

The local tinny house closed then opened the next day…

The drones continued to fly the sky…

"And then," said Vixie, with a sad smile, "I came back home, and guess what, our little lad had commenced droning again even before I left."

"So," said Dixie, "neither method worked your one or the justice system."

Vixie's shoulders slumped.

"You tried your best," said Trixie.

Mixie smiled, put her arm around Vixie. "You gave it your best shot," she said, straight faced.

Nearly every creature in the tree giggled, including Vixie, but not Marmalade, who was trying not to listen, because she knew a certain pixie was able to read her mind.

***

Postscript: The methods used by Vixie to exact justice are totally unacceptable, are against the law and have no moral foundation and is not recommended under any circumstances, even in times of war.

The dangers in shooting a drone from the sky cannot be over emphasised, e.g., smashing through a car wind screen, crashing in a children's playground, taking the washing off a line, the list is endless.

PPS: But it's great fun JA.

***

Well-worn but Worn Well (R16)

Preface: They don't make stuff like they used to.

In the old days before the throwaway society of today stuff was made to last, whether you wanted it too or not.

Author

***

Mixie was standing in front of a full-length mirror. "What do you think?" she asked.

Looking up from the magazine that he was reading, Dixie stared, saying, "What am I supposed to be looking at?"

She twirled. "My pyjamas."

They happened to be in Mixie's room with Dixie lying on her bed propped up by pillows enjoying a restful moment or six before the chaos of another day got underway.

He frowned, puzzled. "Where did you get those, the Op Shop?"

Aghast, hands on her hips, she said, "These PJs were purchased from a quality department store I'll have you know."

He thought about that fact, before saying, "When?"

With a bossy sniff, she said, haughtily, "Year 1963! They have worn well."

Looking at her from head-to-toe Dixie said, "There are holes in the elbow of each sleeve."

She scrutinised the wear and tear and unable to deny the obvious, said, "I am well aware of the damage and will be repairing that area of the garment forthwith."

Dixie thought about the new set of facts for a few seconds before enquiring with interest, "Why bother, we have heaps of moola, just get another pair, and by the way what sort of material is that?"

She primped at the jacket, smoothing the cloth. "This, Dixie, is genuine flannel, not to be mistaken for flannelette." Her look was challenging as she lifted the hem of the jacket, and said, "What do you see, sunshine?"

He looked warily, unsure of what lay before him.

"Well?" she challenged.

"Um, pyjama bottoms," he said, uneasily.

She shook her head slowly. "Yes, but what else?" she asked, her forefinger tapping at her waist…

He knew he was being led up the garden path, ahead of him a minefield of misconceptions and booby traps, so he said, cautiously, "Looks like the ends of a bit of tatty rope."

She bridled, instantly saying, "Tatty rope! This Dixie is genuine woven pyjama cord which has to be tied in a neat bow, what have you got?"

He looked, took a breath, stalled for time, then. "Um, an elastic waist band and buttons," he said, uncertainly.

She smiled at him in a kind way. "I have genuine pyjama cord from way back in the day, not cheap and nasty unreliable elastic."

He nodded. "They don't make PJs like that anymore," he said, reverently.

"Yes," she said, "you're right," giving him her thousand-watt smile.

"Can I get back to reading my magazine now?" he asked.

"Hmm, I still need your help," she said, "I'm thinking about getting my hair cut."

He looked at her almost waist length tresses of whitish blond hair, saying, "That seems a pity, I think it looks great."

"Yeah, I know," she said modestly, "but it becomes a nuisance when we are mixing it with baddies."

"How so?" he asked.

She shrugged. "Well, you know, they grab my hair and there are problems which cramp my style forcing me to kick them in the nuts."

"Ah yeah," he said, "there is that and they end up writhing in agony on the floor and creating an unseemly racket."

"They don't make baddies like they used to, Dixie, and not only that, I have to cut my toenails extra short, which is a bit of a bummer."

He rearranged his pillows before saying, "I don't understand why short toenails?"

Her smile had a hint of malice about it, as she said, "I can get more blunt force trauma with short toenails."

He smiled. "Of course you can."

"Anyway," she said, "how about this?" And quickly arranged her hair into a ponytail.

He pursed his lips thoughtfully. "Yeah, a ponytail may be more difficult to grab…but you could still get your hair cut to, say, just below shoulder length… Hmm, any horse would be proud of it."

She threw a cushion at his head, just as the front door was opened and closed. Then a voice said, "Are you two decent?"

"That's Vixie, we are in my room, come on in," shouted Mixie.

A dishevelled looking pixie peered around the bedroom door cautiously, caught sight of Mixie and said, "What the hell are you wearing?"

"Those things," said Dixie, with due reverence, "are her best PJs which she presents occasionally."

Stepping into the room, Vixie did a head to toe of Mixie, saying, "What are they made of, cardboard?"

Mixie looked around for a cushion…

"She's run out of ammunition," said Dixie.

Vixie's smile was superior, as she said, "When I'm resting, I wear the silk PJ's Trixie gave me."

"Mixie can beat that," said Dixie proudly, "tell her about the vintage cotton cord." And so Mixie regaled her female pixie friend and gang member with the minutiae of woven pyjama cord and its significance in the scheme of social hierarchy.

Vixie sat on the corner of the bed shaking her head, saying, as she looked at Dixie, "I have never heard so much crap in all my life she makes it up."

Which made all three pixies fall about laughing, with Mixie saying eventually, "Anyway, where the hell have you been?"

"Yeah," said Dixie, "and not to put too fine a point on it, Vixie, you pong a bit."

The smelly one scratched her head, with M & D recoiling, as she said, "We have been in, Abilene." She had the look of a relaxed well-travelled warrior.

A thoughtful silence followed Vixie's announcement until, Mixie said, "When you say, Abilene, do you mean the one in America?"

Sitting on the corner of Mixie's bed, Vixie nodded. "Yeah, there was some huge liquor racket that Trixie got involved in."

"Did you find yourselves locked in a cupboard, by any chance?" asked Dixie, with mock politeness.

"No, we did not," said Vixie, with a glare, "but we had to do some undercover work which meant no showers for a week or so."

"Bloody hell, Vixie, you are sitting on my bed," yelled Mixie, "now I'll have to burn it."

"Don't exaggerate," said the secret agent, "I'll have a shower now, but I haven't got any gear with me, not until tomorrow, I think. Don't ask."

"All right," said Mixie, "but get off my bed now, stink-pot, you can have some of my stuff… Go on, get your ass into gear."

Vixie retired as gracefully as possible to the bathroom and M & D could hear her singing rude songs as she scrubbed.

Leaving clothes outside the door, Mixie shouted, "Your filthy infested stuff throw out the window, Dixie can put it in the organic garbage."

"Why me?" came the voice of a much-maligned Dixie.

Mixie smiled to herself. "Because in times of crisis, Dixie, you are the leader."

He shouted back, "Only when you don't want to do it."

"Why are you shouting?" asked Mixie, appearing at the bedroom door. "You're in charge of the organic and I'm in charge of the inorganic."

He looked at his most favourite pixie in the cosmos. "Is clothing organic or inorganic?"

She looked at him through slit eyes. "There is debate about that" – she paused – "tell you what, we'll do it together, you can pick up the infested stuff with that garden fork thing and I'll hold the bin."

"Which bin?" he asked.

She whispered, "The—"

"Right," he said, "not a word about this to anyone."

"You have my pledge and promise, Dixie."

"Okay," he said, "it's a deal."

Poking her head out of the bedroom door, Mixie shouted, "Where's Trixie?"

A muffled voice from the bathroom said, "She had to stay at the Embassy to report, while I was dumped in a taxi."

The duo heard the bathroom door open, with Vixie saying, "I like the logo on the shirt, 'Try to Kiss Me and Die'."

Vixie appeared in the doorway with a flourish. "Ah that, feels better, now about those pyjamas of yours, Mixie, when are we going to burn them?"

"Yes," said Dixie, "we could have an early, Guy Fawkes Day."

Mixie didn't laugh, saying, "These are my forever lasting PJs."

Later, that evening, with the three pixies and Marmalade sitting on the sundeck, with twilight waiting to take everyone by surprise, Dixie said, "Why is the alphabet in that particular order, starting with A?"

A puzzled Vixie, murmured, "What?"

"Well," he said, "after all the most popular and used letter, is E."

Just then, before anyone could reply to Dixie's non-event question the front door was opened, some muttering took place, with Trixie shouting, "I'm here with all our stuff, give me a hand."

"Oh good," said Vixie, "she's in time for the hedgehogs."

"Hmm," grizzled Mixie, "I hope she's had a shower and changed her clothes," as the Chinese pixie appeared at the back door, dressed in an immaculate white linen suit, with shoes to match her eyes.

Afterthoughts:

1. Flannel a soft woollen fabric.
2. Flannelette a cotton imitation of flannel.
3. A Royal Commission of Enquiry is investigating a rearrangement of the alphabet with an estimated time allocation of two point four years at a cost of one hundred million dollars and fifty cents.

***

Another Day in Quasi Land (R16)

Preface: There are many interesting points about pixies one is the fact that they are immune to all human diseases.

However, pixies, like the rest of us, could have problems if they fall under a bus, jump off a cliff, or try to stop a bullet.

So, barring accidents, they go through life bug free for their allotted 150 pixie years.

Author

***

At this moment in space and time, Vixie happens to be very busy tidying the garden with her green fingers, trimming, weeding and talking. Hmm.

While at the same time, two other pixies have just finished their housework, with Mixie remarking that, even in a quasi-world chores still had to be done.

Presently, these two-house keepers were now resting sprawled in an ungainly fashion on their deckchairs, with the luxury of watching another pixie work her butt off.

"The brim on that hat Vixie is wearing," said Mixie, "is so huge all you can see is hat and two skinny legs."

"Yes," agreed Dixie, "a walking sombrero, with a very busy pixie beneath it, who appears to know what she's doing."

"Hmm, that garden bin is nearly full and will need to be put out this Thursday for collection." Mixie had obtained the pickup information from her extra smart triple iPhone which she now placed on a side table.

A precious moment of technological free interruption took place when suddenly the device began to wriggle.

"Here we go," said Dixie, "there's a text arriving forthwith."

Mixie smiled. "I like to see my electronic wonder wriggle, and sometimes I set it up to hop."

She picked up her phone. "Oh it's, Trixie, she's on her way, will be here in about fifteen minutes."

A silence enveloped the peaceful scene, with all creatures great and small, more or less, aware of what they were doing, as Dixie said, "Who is Vixie talking to do you think?"

Their eyes met, as Mixie pulled her funny guessing face. "It wouldn't surprise me if she is talking to the plants," she murmured thoughtfully.

He sighed. "Hmm could be, what about, would you say?"

Gazing into the half distance, Mixie conjectured, "She could be reassuring them that the snipping was like having your toenails cut and that the discomfort would be minimal but essential for their wellbeing."

"Uh huh, that makes sense, because we know for a fact that plants can communicate," he said.

As they watched their volunteer gardener, she suddenly flopped down under the shade of a tree with the hat covering her whole body.

"Isn't that neat!" exclaimed Mixie. "I want a hat like that, Dixie."

He looked at his most favourite pixie is the cosmos, saying, "I think you will have to go to Mexico to get it."

With a grumpy frown, Mixie said, "Oh no, I could find myself hiding in a cupboard being chased by baddies."

"Yeah," he said, "forget it, there's no dignity in that."

They heard the front door open and close, with Trixie shouting, "I've arrived and to prove it I'm here."

"You're early," said Dixie, "what are you going to do now?"

"Yes," Mixie, informed their oriental companion, "we are on the sundeck watching another pixie work it is great entertainment."

"Um, I'm going in the shower first then I'll join you in the front row," was the reply.

Eight minutes five seconds later, Trixie appeared at the back door.

"Wow!" said Mixie. "Don't you look a million dollars."

Trixie twirled and posed in a simple white cotton dress ending just below the knee, shoeless, she was the epitome of casual elegance.

"Where did that little number come from?" asked Dixie. "I haven't seen that one before."

"No," said Trixie, settling in her deckchair and demurely arranging her dress, "I found it in the back of a locker at the embassy, must have put it there yonks ago."

With that, the entrepreneur let her eyes wander over the garden…

"What do you think, Trixie?" asked Mixie.

"Yes, Vixie knows what she's doing, is that her under the hat?"

"We think so," said Dixie.

The quietness of the afternoon was broken by Vixie sitting up with the hat tumbling to one side, as she shouted, "I thought that was you, informing us loudly, about your arrival where did you get the dress at the Sallies?"

They all fell about laughing, with Marmalade making an abrupt about turn as she came onto the sundeck… *It's going to be one of those afternoons,* she thought.

As the pixies gathered together once again their equilibrium, Vixie said, "I put some clean water down for the hedgehogs, poor things and that garden bin is chocka."

"We know, we know, it gets put out this Thursday," said Dixie.

It was then, as the three pixies relaxed quietly for a moment or two, lost in their own thoughts, that they witnessed a scene which was uncanny but beautiful at the same time.

As Vixie sat in the shade of the tree several birds fluttered down from their leafy refuge and began to peck and hop up close and personal to the resting pixie.

She then began to talk to her avian visitors…

"Hey, you two," said Mixie, quietly, "are you seeing what I'm seeing?"

"Ah yes," Trixie murmured, "our little battler can charm the birds out of the trees if she puts her mind to it."

"Really," Dixie noisily shifted his chair to get a better ring side seat, "how does she…"

Trixie cut him off, saying, "Shush, just watch."

And sure enough, as the four onlookers (which now included an entranced cat), observed the phenomenon with Vixie, obviously speaking to her winged guests; the birds hopped on her arms, fingers, and one cutie even balanced on her big toe.

"That is astonishing," whispered Mixie.

In hushed tones, Trixie said, "There are many sides to, Vixie."

They watched, they listened, but even the super hearing of the pixies couldn't pick up what was being said.

It was then that Dixie murmured, thoughtfully, "I wonder if this sort of behaviour could be attributed to what happened to Vixie during the war?"

A glance passed between the two female pixies, as Trixie said, "The loss of her partner during that time had a profound effect on her, in my nonprofessional opinion, and is the cause of her sometimes-erratic behaviour."

With that, Vixie obviously said something to her friends, donned her hat once again and ambled towards the pixies, saying, "Are we up for our session with the hedgehogs later?" Flopped in her deckchair and threw her hat at Dixie.

"Absolutely," he said, "I wonder if they would eat a bit of cat food?"

As Marmalade stalked off in disgust, Vixie brightened, saying, "They will if I give it to them."

"You can be the official hedgehog minder from now on, all in favour say aye," said Mixie.

There were four resounding shouts of aye, with Marmalade abstaining in high dudgeon.

As the pixies relaxed waiting for the twilight hour to make up its mind to put in an appearance, a tranquil silence enveloped the sundeck and environs, broken by Trixie saying, "I've been thinking."

Six eyes settled on the Chinese millionaire waiting to be enlightened about her thoughts.

After a moment or two, Dixie said, "What about?"

With her eyes shut to indicate thoughtfulness, Trixie said, "About pixie existence and nonexistence."

"What about it?" asked Mixie.

"Well," said Trixie, "the other day, I was trying to work out the different times of our comings and goings."

"Hmm, I'm pretty sure that I was the first out of the four of us, I remember waking up in a strawberry patch," said Mixie.

"Yeah," Trixie nodded, as details started to drift back, "that's right, it was 1904, I think. What about you, Dixie?"

"Um, wow, so much time and so many things have happened over the years, it was 1912, I think." He looked at Mixie for confirmation.

She nodded. "Yes, that must have been a vintage year," Mixie said, with a smile.

"Before you ask," said Vixie, "I'm the youngest of us four, 1916, and you Trixie the year of the pixie in 1914, or something like that."

"Why do you ask?" said Mixie.

Trixie looked towards the garden with its now neatly trimmed back and sides, saying thoughtfully, "I read an interesting article the other day, which I think gives us a clue to our longevity."

If she didn't already have the full attention of the other pixies, Trixie now had it in spades.

Immediately, Vixie said, "That could be part of our pixie-mania research."

"Exactly," agreed Trixie, as she was interrupted by a caterwauling howl coming from the front of the house, followed by yelps and a man swearing…

Vixie said, with a big smile, "Good on you, Marmalade, she's just stopped another pisser in his tracks, that cat is definitely a pixie."

They fell about laughing, until Dixie said, "Where were we?" As Marmalade came around the corner of the house, thinking, *I wonder if this lot could organise a steak dinner in a meat works?*

"Ah, yes," said Trixie, "the article."

"Yeah, tell us about that," said Vixie, followed by, "just a tick, I'll get my laptop to add some info to the data bank."

As the pixies settled once again, with Marmalade under the table, not listening, Trixie said, "Well, the part that interested me the most suggested some species rarely get sick from various viruses, because of their unique immune system."

Trixie waited, letting the penny drop, as the saying goes.

The note taker spoke first, saying, "Ah that is interesting, it could mean pixies have such an immune system."

Again, there was a long silence, during which birds bedded down, while hedgehogs discussed their upcoming evening out with drinks.

The silence was so long Marmalade checked to see if the pixies were still alive.

They were, with Vixie saying, "Leave it with me, I'll follow up on the details later."

"That's good," said Trixie, "I'll hunt out that article for you."

Whilst under the table, Marmalade thought… *Are we in line for another thousand-page memo, I must remember to be out that day?*

***

That evening, the pixies made their way garden end wise armed with a small can of cat food, watched from the sundeck by a sulking feline.

As the pixies settled under a kowhai tree they watched closely as Vixie placed a small portion of cat food beside the water bowl.

They waited, looking at the stars, with Mixie thinking… *There's a scrap of star dust in all of us…*

As Trixie said, "I wonder if there is any gold worth having on the moon do you think?"

With Dixie saying, "Huh, I don't see why not, why, are you thinking of an expedition?"

Her blue eyes twinkled as the pixie best dresser, said, "I just might do that one of these days."

"Be quiet you lot," growled Vixie, "I think we have movement."

Sure enough, two prickly companions trundled out from under the hedge and did a jerky kind of bumble towards the water bowl.

Then, the spiky ones hesitated, changed direction slightly as they headed for the cat food first, with Vixie speaking softly to her four-legged friends.

"She's a hedgehog whisperer," said Mixie.

As it turned out, the hogs were extremely interested in cat food and scoffed the whole can of gourmet minced steak and lamb cutlets.

"Are you going to tickle their tummies," asked Dixie.

"No, I am not," said Vixie, "these little creatures will be treated with dignity, or you will be answerable to me, if not."

There was a collective, "Hmm," as Trixie rearranged her hair with her fingers and smoothed the creases from her frock.

She then said, "By the way, I would like to get your permission to volunteer the four of us to follow up on a Russian Mafia investigation."

Even the hedgehogs looked askance not believing what they had just heard.

For some reason, Vixie sat up to attention, the can of cat food dropping from her nerveless fingers.

At the same time, Dixie not quite believing what he had just heard, waited.

As for the hedge dwellers, they scuttled home, pleased they were not pixies.

Dixie, finally said, "Sorry, Trixie, I wasn't paying attention did you say something about the Russian Mafia."

The Chinese super-agent smiled gently. "We need the dynamic foursome on this golden opportunity."

Mixie, who hadn't really been listening at all, because of her preoccupation with star dust, said, "Are we going to a Russian ballet, which one?"

Whereas, Vixie, who listened to everything, said, "Will we be armed to the teeth and beyond?"

"I'm sure we will have all the bells and whistles," Trixie informed her teammate.

"Will we have piano wire?" growled Vixie.

"Piano wire?" asked Mixie, yet to arrive back to the reality of a quasi-world. "Are we going into the piano business?"

"No! The piano wire is for garrotting the enemy, quickly and quietly," said a very informative Vixie.

"Just a minute, just a cotton-picking minute, can we start over again," yelled Dixie, getting himself in a tizzy, "what's this all about?"

"Well," said Trixie, coolly and calmly, "the Russian Mafia may be in this country as we speak and we are going to start looking under blankets, sort of thing to see what's going on."

Finally, Mixie fell back to earth with a metaphorical thump, "What's this!?" she shouted. "The bloody Russians are worse than the American Mafioso, they take no prisoners and shoot the wounded."

Vixie smiled coyly. "That sounds like me," she said sweetly, "perhaps I should change sides."

Glowering at the best dresser in pixie land, but at the same time trying to hide a smile, shaking her head, Mixie said, "You know we are suckers for this type of shindig, right Dixie?"

"We are?" he said, followed by, "Of course we are, bring it on!"

Marmalade, who had been listening all the while, thought, *This lot would have problems organising an ice cream from an ice cream vendor…*

So, back on the sundeck, all five cogitated about the proposal put forward by, Trixie, with Dixie being the first to speak.

He leaned forward with an intelligent frown creasing his forehead, and said, "There is an obvious need to plan this totally important disaster we are about to embark upon."

They all nodded sagely except for Marmalade, who sighed.

"Tell you what," said Mixie, leaping to her feet, "the night is fine, the grass will be damp underfoot, how about we go for a walk and devise a cunning plan, on route?"

So that's what they all decided, except Marmalade who did not look forward to the dreaded wet paws syndrome, but went anyway, thinking… *I have a feeling in my bones this farce can only end in disaster.*

They left the lights on, locked the place up tight, ambled, talked and connived.

The night sky was indeed clear, stars ablaze, the universe expanding despite its natural desire after an explosion to fall in on itself and end the whole farcical charade…

Vixie was at that point in time trying to hammer home her request for automatic weapons, when there was a distant popping sound.

A few seconds later, a silent green cloud of unbreakable gossamer enveloped the strolling pixies.

And the more the pixies struggled against the cloying mass the more enmeshed they became.

"We got them," said a heavily accented voice.

This claim was followed immediately by Trixie saying, "Boris, what brings you back?"

Then, out of the darkness strolled a tall woman dressed in a skin-tight black leather trouser suit, who said, "Are you sure we have all of the little bastards?"

Her accent was also fractured but accompanied by an attractive lisp.

The leather person's presence was immediately acknowledged by Trixie saying, "Olga, as well?"

In the meantime, as chance would have it, Vixie and Marmalade had fortuitously escaped the dreaded cloying green cloud and melted into the surrounding darkness; a ploy not as easy as it sounds.

In answer to Olga's question about the little bastards, Boris counted, using his fingers. "Bugger!" he said. "There's one missing."

An evil smirk crossed Olga's handsome face, as she said, "That one will come crawling back when she learns of what we intend for our captives to make them talk."

With a puzzled frown, Boris said, "How will the missing pixie learn of what we intend to do to the other three?"

Olga smiled, at her, thick as two short planks partner. "We'll use the grapevine," she said.

"Are there grapes at this time of the year?" Boris asked, sincerely.

The karate expert sighed heavily… "Let's get going," she said, with sadness in her voice.

The three helpless pixies were quickly bundled into a dark painted panel van and whisked on their way in a trice.

With a stunned sniff, Vixie said, from her perch in a nearby tree, "Marmalade, we have an interesting and challenging few hours ahead of us."

The cat, sitting by her side, thought… *This is not going to end well…*

Retrieving her triple iPhone from her back pocket Vixie scrawled and poked, saying casually, "There they are, Marmalade, heading northeast," and shoved the phone under the cat's nose.

The feline looked and saw a red dot moving along a blue line and wondered what was happening.

"You are probably wondering what is happening, right Marmalade?" said Vixie.

Oh no! Thought the cat. *Another one of them that can tell what I'm thinking, how do they do it?*

Smiling, Vixie said, as she flicked on an illumination device in her triple I, she held it to her ear and pulled back a pixie lobe. "See that," she said, pointing.

Marmalade squinted and saw a small bump under the skin of the pixie warrior.

"That is a transponder, and Trixie has the same implanted device, we know within a metre where each other are at all times."

Wow, thought the cat… *I'll go to the bottom of our garden these pixies are something else…*

"Thing is, Marmalade, that Olga pest will know that I intend to make a rescue attempt." Vixie paused thinking, before continuing, "And I would say there will be more than two of them to deal with."

The early morning silence was profound it was cooler, the grass wetter, and the stars brighter, but still a long way from sparrow fart that van is heading. *It's a long way to walk...* thought Marmalade.

Vixie smiled at the cat, saying, "You are probably thinking that it's a long way to follow that van."

A despairing Marmalade thought... *I give up...*

"Thing is, we will not be walking, running or skipping to the rescue, Marmalade, we will be travelling by a secret embassy car but first let us check out the baddies final destination and slide by the house to see what's happening."

As they passed the villa, Vixie said, "Uh oh, the front door is open, one good thing though, Marmalade, I totalled the computer within seconds of the abduction with my triple i smart phone."

The cat looked sadly at the swinging gate and its saturated past wondering would they ever be able to return?

"You may be wondering about going back to the house," said Vixie, "I think that most unlikely."

At this moment in time, Marmalade was no longer surprised by, Vixie's Ouija Board mind reading capabilities, as they proceeded to wait outside the dairy for the embassy car.

The vehicle turned out to be a black nondescript fade into the background remember-less motorway hack, which purred at the kerb like a cat on steroids; whilst Vixie popped into the shop and bought some cat lollies.

"You are probably hungry," she said, to the cat, as Marmalade thought, *You can read my mind...*

Getting into the car, Vixie said, "Hi, Gil, here we go again."

The driver smiled and that's all he said.

"Here's our destination," she said, handing Gil her device.

He nodded, and saying no more, was on the way.

Arriving at the tidal inlet, Vixie noted that no houses occupied the area, whereas there were several boat sheds in the vicinity.

"Dollars to doughnuts they'll be in one of those sheds," she murmured to herself.

Gil nodded his agreement but didn't elaborate.

Letting a thoughtful puff of air escape, her eyes narrowed, as she said softly, "Gil, wait in the next street for half an hour if you get an ABC message, stick around to pick us up; if nothing return to the embassy."

He nodded and remained silent.

"Do not get involved," she said.

Gil remained silent, drove away and parked, continuing to read, 'War and Peace' by a guy named, Leo Tolstoy, who he thought had promise as a writer, although a little long-winded.

"Come on, Marmalade, that van will probably be parked at the back of one of these sheds."

And so it was, with Marmalade's fur bristling at the sight.

"When we enter you have only one thing to do," said Vixie, a talker to animals, "you aim for the woman, Olga, and plant yourself firmly with claws extended in the middle of her back."

I can do that, thought Marmalade… *Why did I think this was going to be difficult…*

Creeping up to a side door, which Vixie knew would be unlocked, the perfect trap, she opened it quickly and glided inside.

"Ah," said Olga warmly, "we meet at—"

Before Olga could get any further, Marmalade planted herself firmly in the middle of Olga's back, digging in like there was no tomorrow.

The scream from Olga was somewhat muffled as she tried desperately to remove the cat with razor sharp claws, that was tantalisingly out of her reach.

The three pixies were chained in one corner of the shed, guarded by two hulking bozos, with Boris sitting at a small table trying to read a map, which was upside down.

A smile crossed Vixie's face. "Is this all I've got to deal with," she whispered to herself.

In the split seconds that followed, a glance passed between all four pixies as the captives lunged forward kicking the two guards in the back of their knees.

As the bozos began to crumple forward, Vixie withdrew an automatic pistol from the back pocket of her jeans. "Which one of you would like to be first, it would be my pleasure to choose if you can't make your mind up."

She swept the pistol in an arc to include the map reader.

Not one of the baddies accepted her invitation.

"Keys," she demanded from Boris.

He didn't move, whereas Olga appeared to be performing a strange South American dance.

"Give her the ******* keys," screamed Olga.

Boris fumbled the keys from a pocket, threw them at Vixie, who deftly caught them, tossing their means of escape to Mixie.

Releasing the chains all three pixies accidently stepped on the faces of the bozos as they apologised for being in the way.

"Put them all in chains," said Vixie, "they can give each other a cuddle, oh yes you can hop off now, Marmalade."

Is that an order? the cat thought.

"That is an order," said Vixie.

"Chains?" queried Dixie, giving Vixie a 'look'.

She smiled. "No, of course not, I think the pixie hog tie would be far more appropriate."

Retrieving some coils of rope that were hanging on the wall of the shed the pixies set to work, whilst Vixie put a call through to, Gil.

During the truss pull, truss pull procedure, Trixie said to their rescuer, "You realise the pixie hog tie is contrary to various Geneva protocols, they will need to be given the appropriate warnings."

Askance, Vixie said, "What!"

With a smile, Trixie looked at their knotted guests. "I know the rules off by heart, let me be their teacher."

She then proceeded with some helpful advice for the neatly trussed up prisoners…

"If you sneeze, you will strangle yourself. If you cough, the same thing, if you yawn ditto, and if you fart, your demise is instant do I make myself clear?"

The prisoners glowered.

"I'll take that as a yes," she said.

As Gil came in, he asked, "Which are the Russians?" in a very cultured voice.

Vixie pointed. "Those two, the others are local bozos."

Looking down at Boris, Gil, said, "Do you know anything about, Leo Tolstoy?"

Boris frowned. "There was a Leo I knew once that ran a vodka joint," he mumbled.

Even Olga had to smile, in Russian, of course.

With that, Trixie got in touch with the appropriate authorities and the pixies waited in the shadows to ensure the arrest of the hapless four.

Once in the car, Vixie explained about the ransacking of pixie villa.

Mixie and Dixie held hands in silence as Trixie said, "You will all be staying with me at the embassy, I have a suite of rooms there, then we'll get all this sorted."

And that's what happened, among many other things…

***

1. Notes which may be of interest:
2. Never feed cat food to hedgehogs it gives them acne, check it out.
3. Talk to your plants and animals they are living flora and fauna with feelings.
4. So called 'bad language' is merely human language but be sparing in its use lest it lose impact.
5. Violence of any kind is to be avoided, yeah right.
6. The gun Vixie used was a realistic toy.
7. Marmalade was awarded a medal for, Outstanding Bravery, and a lifetime of cat lollies.
8. Olga and Boris were moved through diplomatic channels (again), more painful than it sounds.
9. Only to be replaced by two other 'diplomats' of interest.
10. The world of espionage and things that go bump in the night is convoluted like a sack of worms A short hiatus.

***

The Smoking Man

Preface: Home is where the heart is or maybe the mind come to think of it. Is there any difference in the long run?

Author

***

With an officious shake of her head, the office manager said, "Have you seen a cat running around here?" The cleaner looked at the OM from his vantage point of a step ladder, as he dusted the President's portrait.

"No, any way cats are not allowed in the embassy, you best go see security."

With a deep long-suffering sigh, the OM said, "I did that and Gil told me the same as you, but added that cats could be wired and pose a security risk."

Sitting under a, chaise longue, out of sight, Marmalade thought... *I haven't seen a wired cat, what are they talking about?*

***

Meanwhile, sitting at a solid teak table in her suite of rooms was Trixie, three other pixies, Gil and Tilley, the millionaire's personal assistant.

"So, what's the verdict, Gil?" asked Trixie.

Gil's reply was thoughtful, conscious of the feelings of M & D, as he said, "Your place is in pristine condition, not a thing out of place, however."

"Uh oh," said Dixie, "what does the, however, mean?"

"It means," continued Gil, "that I have not seen a more professional job of bugging a place in the whole of my career."

Looking intensely at the head of security, her mauve eyes causing even a professional like Gil a tad of uneasiness, Mixie said, "Just give us the guts of the situation."

"Your place," he said precisely, "is uninhabitable in my opinion even the tap washers are bugged."

"So, any thought of debugging, over time," said Tilley, "is out of the question?"

Gil nodded. "Yeah, we couldn't guarantee a one hundred percent operation even the garden hose has devices implanted."

A silence, broken by Trixie saying, "Knock the whole place down and start again, I can tell you right now, money is no object."

"That will have to be done anyway for selling purposes, and for normal use would have been okay, but not how the premises are used at present," said Gil.

"Hmm, all right," said Trixie thoughtfully, "how about start again somewhere else."

All eyes settled on Mixie and Dixie, with Tilley eventually saying, "Somewhere new, with everything built to your specifications."

The two pixies held hands, their eyes met, as Dixie gave the slightest nod, with Mixie saying, "I think we can live with that."

***

And that, as they say, is precisely what happened.

A large section of land was procured, a bit native bushy, a bit grassy, a bit out of the way...

Where a new dwelling was built with a slightly 'used' look at the request of M & D, allowing for a games room under the house, shingle roof, a villa fit for a couple of semi-retired pixies.

However, while all this was being achieved the delightful duo and others still managed to become involved in an escapade or six. Just to keep our hand in, as Mixie explained.

***

Meantime, life at the embassy continued as per normal with four pixies and an unofficial cat in residence, but as Trixie explained, living in luxury is nowhere near as nice as having a home of your own.

On this particular day, a Saturday, three pixies were sitting in the luxurious lounge not really watching, 'War of The Worlds' when Tilley appeared at the door.

"Well," she said, laughing, "I have never seen such a disconsolate group of creatures in the whole of my puff."

"Uh, tell us you have come to rescue three bored out of their skull pixies," growled Vixie.

Standing in front of the TV, nodding wisely, Tilley, the PA, said, "I have indeed."

"Yippee!" shouted the three in unison and performed cartwheels, walked on their hands and hovered in the air touching fingers for a few seconds with legs outstretched much to the astonishment of Tilley.

"Where are we going?" asked a breathless, Dixie.

Tilley pulled a face. "Well it's not a big deal, but anything is better than being stuck in here, right?"

"Absolutely," said Mixie, "get us out of this luxurious prison."

"Well," said the PA, "there is a new shopping mall over at, Mt Eden, which is a bit different, being built in a manner that suits the district, that is, not big bold and brassy, everything in good taste, and with due respect to two-dollar stores, there are none."

"Let's go," said Vixie, "and lower the tone."

Everyone fell about laughing.

"Besides that," said Tilley, "I have booked to get my hair done, while you guys can look around the mall."

"What are you going to have done to your hair?" asked Vixie.

Tilley looked at the pixies, shaking her head, and said, "You guys are very nosey little creatures, which gets you into all sorts of trouble."

"Correct," said Mixie, with her thousand-watt smile, "and we love it, now, what are you going to have done with your hair?"

Laughing in disbelief, but with good humour, Tilley said, "Shortened."

The pixies circled Tilley, with Vixie saying, "What do you think of that, Dixie?"

"Hmm." He nodded, in total confidence. "As long as it's not too far above the collar."

The three pixies looked at a perplexed, PA, waiting.

Who, again, in disbelief, said, "That is exactly what I intend to have done?"

"We rest our case," said the pixies in unison.

"Come on you little buggers, my car is under the house," said a bemused, Tilley.

"We need to take a cushion each so that we can see out of the windows," Dixie explained.

***

Leading the way, Tilley said, pointing, "That's my car over there."

The pixies stared, with Mixie finally saying, "Hmm, very nice, what colour is that?"

"Pearl white, I think," said Tilley, opening up, "it's easy to keep clean."

"Can I please sit in the front?" asked Dixie, politely.

The female pixies eyes met, with a wink, Mixie saying, "Let the child sit in the front."

"Yes," said her counterpart, "or he may throw a tantrum."

Dixie's look said…I'll get you two later…

"Okay," explained Tilley, "you know the drill."

"Yes, yes," said Vixie, "belt up and shut up."

As their journey to the mall proceeded, Tilley said, "Look at that, two young people helping an old lady cross the street, isn't that sweet."

Dixie looked over his shoulder, saying, "I'll phone it in, there could be a patrol car nearby."

"Okay," said Mixie, "I'll let you know which way they're heading."

"What are you two gabbling on about?" asked Tilley.

Dixie's voice was sad. "Those two kids filched the lady's purse from her handbag."

Tilley half swung around to Vixie, at the same time expertly missing six cyclists, "Did you see that?"

"Yes," she said, "watch out for the bus."

A few pixie seconds ticked by…

Mixie's phone burped, she looked, scrolled. "Good one, there was a patrol car close by they picked up the kids the lady will soon have her purse back."

There was silence in the car for a moment or three before, Tilley said, "I wonder what will happen to those children?"

Three pixies considered Tilley's question for a moment, before one said, "Maybe the purse fell out of her bag by accident."

"Fat chance," said the second.

"Maybe pigs will fly," said the third.

With a sigh, Tilley said, "She could have been their grandma."

Silence once again within the metal and plastic carriage, before Tilley continued with, "What sort of device have you got Dixie, whereby you can get onto a police frequency immediately?"

"Ah," said M & D in unison.

"What does, ah, mean please explain," asked Tilley, swerving carefully to avoid a dog crossing the road, oblivious of the traffic.

Vixie smiled, twitching her eyebrows at the duo, "You won't get an answer out of those two they worked closely with AOS, back in the day on special assignments."

"AOS?" asked Tilley.

"Armed Offenders Squad," replied Vixie, leaving a previous lifetime of things unsaid.

Tilley had become silent and thoughtful as she pulled in the parking lot, looking at the pixies with a new respect and a zillion questions that were going to be unanswered, meantime.

As she got out of the car, Tilley said, "I'm going for lunch after my hair appointment, then to the bank for a meeting with the manager re some business for, Trixie."

As the pixies piled out of the car, Vixie said, "Yeah, where is Trixie these days?"

Tilley looked at the three pixies in a group as sweet as, saying, "Trixie is in, Ankara, something to do with shipbuilding and textiles."

"We'll never keep up with that pixie," said Mixie as they entered the mall.

"Keep out of trouble you three," said Tilley, heading for the hairdressers.

Dixie looked askance at his trouble- makers- in- arms colleague. "Don't we always," he said, as they giggled their way into the mall.

***

"Where to first?" asked Mixie?

"Well, I would like to look around the library and pick up a library card," he said, "how about you, Vixie?"

She nodded. "Yeah, that's fine by me."

Mixie looked at her favourite pixie. "If you get a card, I want one, too."

He thought about that for a second or two. "What for?"

Taking a bunch of cards out of her back pocket, Mixie said, "Dixie, Dixie, Dixie, you just don't understand about cards, it's the amount one collects, not what they are for."

He looked, frowned, then said, "Amongst that lot you've got, a plumber, electrician, drain layer, gardeners, an obstetrician, what?"

The card holder smiled kindly. "That is neither here nor there, the point is I will eventually be able to flash heaps of cards and people and pixies can eat their hearts out, right Vixie?"

The only other female pixie in the mall let out a puff of air. "I give in," she said simply, throwing up her arms in despair.

As they entered the library, Dixie said, "You will forever be a mystery, Mixie."

She gave him a sideways hug. "You are so lucky to have me."

Nobody looked up as the pixies made their way to the counter, with Vixie saying, "People take very little notice of us these days."

The librarian greeted the pixies with a smile. "You must be the new-fangled robots that are out and about these days… Wow your skin is very realistic."

"Oh yes," said Vixie, sweetly, with an edge, "it's made of a new material called, elastaplex."

The other two pixies tried not to smile.

"How can I help you?" asked the librarian her name was Cynthia, according to her identification tag.

"Um, we are interested in getting a library card, Cynthia," said Dixie, politely.

Cynthia smiled benignly upon the pixies. "Really, I didn't know robots could actually read the written word outside of a computer."

Giving the librarian that lop sided dangerous grin, Vixie said, "It's amazing what we are programmed to do these days, I can even put on my own knickers."

It was obvious that Cynthia was taken aback by the mention of a nether garment, so Dixie quickly said, "Tell you what, we'll leave it for now, Cynthia, and pick up some cards another day."

As the pixies left the library bursting at the seams and trying not to roll on the floor in a paroxysm of laughter, Mixie said, between guffaws, "I'm going to buy one of those wallets that hold a hundred cards, if I can find one."

As the pixies began to flit hither and yon taking in all the shops, pointing and chattering, Dixie stopped abruptly.

"What is it," asked Mixie, "something wrong, Dixie?"

He pointed. "There's a guy over there smoking."

She laughed. "Not on fire yet, I hope."

"No, no, this is serious, Mixie, look he's puffing on a cigarette."

"Here we go," said Vixie, "where's security when we need them?"

Shrugging, Dixie said, "Probably dealing with shoplifters."

Three pairs of pixie eyes met, mauve, green and amber. "How about we go over to the gentleman and ask him politely to forego his filthy and dangerous habit?" suggested Vixie.

"Tell you what, you two do that," said Dixie, "while I go drum up security, they can't be too far away, oh yeah, try and leave him in one piece."

"Okay," said Mixie, "off you go, I'm sure the smoking man will be reasonable, right Vixie?"

"How could he resist our charm?" the vixen smiled warmly.

The two pixies drifted towards the offending and offensive gentleman, who happened to be leaning against a fire extinguisher, above which was a notice upon which was printed – NO SMOKING IN THE MALL OR ENVIRONS – THIS IS PRIVATE PROPERTY.

"Good morning, sir," said Mixie, giving him her devastating smile, "you may not have seen the notice above your head about the ban on smoking in the mall."

The smoking man looked at the pixies hovering at nose height their eyes had a glitter about them that made him feel uneasy.

However, with his usual subtle approach in such situations, he said, "Who the hell are you, some tin pot security gadget, f…off."

Mixie's smile grew more intense, while Vixie showed her teeth when she grinned, the smoking man urgently needed to pee, not knowing why.

"There is no need to use offensive language, mister… What is your name, sir?" asked Vixie in a deadly sweet voice.

"Get lost, couple of tin Lizzie's this is a free country. I'll smoke where I like," he said, unsurely.

"Ah," said Mixie quietly, "we don't seem to have got your attention, sir." And with that statement, the pixies split up, moving to the left and right of the smoking man.

His eyes swung wildly left and right as the pixies switched positions in so doing, he smacked his nose with considerable force on the fire extinguisher.

"Shit!" he said, not watching his language. "That really hurt," as his nose began to leak.

"Do you have a hankie, sir, to stem your bodily fluid?" asked Vixie, in a business-like manner.

Just then a voice said, "Having a spot of trouble, are we?" The security guard was massive swamping the smoking man with the trembling yellow fingers and a twitch.

"I. I. I," stuttered the bleeding man, touching his tender nose and lip. "Those robots hit me."

The SG laughed. "What, those two little sweethearts, they'd give you a kiss not a biff."

The two sweethearts blushed and smiled coyly, with Dixie having to turn away before he puked.

The yellow fingered man shook his head completely bewildered. "What the hell are you talking about, I've been assaulted," he lied.

"Please come with me, sir," said the SG politely. "I'll need to take down your particulars, ah yes here come the police as we speak."

Turning to the pixies, the security guard, whose name was, Sandra, added, "Thank you for your assistance; we were busy rounding up our regular shop lifters."

As they walked away, Sandra suggested to the yellow fingered smoking man that he get his bent nose examined as it could be broken and not to walk into fire extinguishers in the future.

"Well," said Mixie, "so much for that."

As they piled into the car, Tilley said, "I hear there was some sort of kerfuffle at the mall."

"Oh that," said Mixie quickly, "security caught their regular bunch of shop lifters, who they said would be back next week, during a break in their community service."

Tilley shook her head. "Yes, they are everywhere these days and well organised."

Silence, as Tilley skilfully missed a group of tourists getting off a coach, talking, pointing and wandering across the road, totally unaware of any traffic.

Mixie said casually, "The security also caught a guy smoking and handed him over the police."

"Those idiots never give up," said Tilley.

"What the police?" Dixie asked.

They all laughed as the rain began to bucket down.

Then Dixie said, "That haircut Tilley, is perfect, it just bounces on your collar as you walk." Tilley couldn't understand for the life of her why she enjoyed that compliment so much… Mixie sighed, looked out the window and contemplated the future in their new place.

***

The Woman with the CF

Preface: Activities at the embassy were running according to, one hopes some form of plan, but diplomacy as with espionage has deceptive cul-de-sacs and endless roads…

There were the usual daily hiccups, with staff swearing on a stack of the good book that they had seen a cat, whose 'wiring' status was unknown.

As for M & D's new place that was on schedule because of the outstanding fine summer, the only hiccup at this stage being the excavation and refilling of an old rabbit warren.

The other interesting occurrence involved, Tilley, who the pixies had learned was quite skilled in unarmed combat.

Now, there just happened to be an embassy gymnasium, hmm.

Anyway, the pixies now looked upon Tilley in a whole new light.

What they saw was a woman in her late twenties, with a PhD in something or other, of average height and weight, BUT, under the business suit quite an athletic deportment.

The five practiced together, learned together, trusted each other and established a bond which could auger well for future escapades with Tilley blissfully unaware in the meantime.

Author

So, where was everybody?

Let's see, Vixie for reasons not explained had joined Trixie in, Istanbul, don't ask…

Tilley was holding the fort at the embassy (her words), while on this warm, sunny and lazy day M & D were reflecting the weather as they relaxed on the small balcony leading from the lounge.

A fantail fluttered onto the rail of the balcony for mere seconds before flying up and over the roof as Tilley stuck her head out of the door, saying, "Try not to overdo it, we don't want you suffering from heat stroke."

The two smiled benignly as Dixie, said, "We just saw the cutest bird with a fan tail, but it has gone now."

"Ah yes," said Tilley, "there used to be heaps of those birds at a place called, Tahuna Torea, nature reserve, but much fewer these days."

The pixies eyes met, with Dixie saying, "Never heard of the place."

Mixie sat up, resting on her elbows, as she looked up at Tilley, "Where is this magic kingdom, this lost place?"

Ignoring the drama, Tilley said, "It's about thirty minutes or so from here, with a beach, bush walks and great view, lovely place."

The mauve met the green, with Mixie saying, "So when are you going to take us, Tilley?"

"Not today, that's for sure, we could think about tomorrow, Saturday."

"You're on!" shouted the pixies in unison. "We'll be ready and waiting."

***

Arriving at, Tahuna Torea, in her car, Tilley instantly found a parking space that had just been vacated and expertly backed in.

Getting out of the car, Mixie said immediately, "This is a nice spot, it's got a bit of everything, beach, bush walks, shallow water for the littlies."

"Come on, let's go," said Tilley, "I know of a grassy knoll under a shady tree further along the beach."

Arriving at the knoll that appeared to be reserved for Tilley and company, the pixies perched themselves in the lower branches of the convenient tree.

As Tilley unpacked her picnic lunch and placed it on a colourful blanket, Mixie said, "While you're stuffing your face, Tilley, let me tell you about a story I'm writing."

Tilley stopped mid-munch and mumbled, "You writing a story, since when?"

"Since I bought this," announced Mixie, withdrawing a device from her back pocket.

Dixie, taken by surprise, said, "I haven't seen that before, what have you got there?"

Mixie smiled upon her companions, saying, "This is a GPX Special, bought it yesterday."

"What has that got to do with you writing a story?" asked Tilley, as she got stuck into an apple square.

With a shrug, Mixie said, "I just talk to it and this little beauty does everything else, like correcting my grammar spelling and can even repair a split infinitive, whatever that is."

A mutter came from Dixie, "That GPX thingy is going to be very busy."

"I heard that, Dixie," said Mixie with a glare.

"Does it do anything else?" asked Tilley.

With a superior look, the female pixie intoned with exaggerated patience, "This amazing thingy has nine hundred and ninety Apps, beat that!"

"Which do what?" enquired Tilley, taking a deep swig of instant.

"I have no idea," said Mixie, "Tilley, you can help me sort out that stuff."

"Oh cool," said the PA, raising her eyebrows derisively, "I get to play with Mixie's new toy, by the way how much did it cost?"

"Ah," said Mixie, deeply.

"What does a deep ah mean?" asked Dixie, with squinty eyes.

Sighing slowly and patiently in frustration Mixie said, "We have heaps of money in the bank, Dixie, but we never spend any, so I thought I'd get the ball rolling, sort of speak."

"Oh yeah, how much?" persisted the pixie with green eyes.

"Um, let me see," she said, "with ten percent discount, because I paid cash, it was one thousand nine hundred and ninety-nine dollars, with a carrying case, good a?"

Tilley stopped sipping her coffee…

Dixie fell out of the tree…

Birds stopped chirping, no they didn't…

The tide went out, no it didn't…

Tilley said slowly, "Does it tell your future?"

"It probably could," said Mixie, with her thousand-watt smile.

Thoughtfully, Dixie asked, "Tell me, what does the GPX stand for?"

Another smile from the budding author. "Genius Phone Xtra, there's not many of them in the world, but they'll catch on."

"Does it do other stuff?" asked Dixie, hopefully.

She looked at her other half, nodding with a sigh. "Of course it does for example it can display what the weather is like on the far side of the moon."

"Hmm, that's handy" – Tilley's tone was drily ironic – "anything else?"

With a superior look, Mixie said, "I can tell you what the housing market is like in a place called, Timbuktu, and what our money is worth in Inuit currency."

Tilley nodded. "Imagine that, it's amazing."

Life appeared to take a pause as seagulls began to swoop and stand around hoping for a handout, as Tilley nodded in understanding. "So, tell us about the story you're writing."

"Glad you asked, let's get to the more important stuff," said Mixie, "my story happens to be a fairy tale."

"Okay," said Tilley, "that is a subject in which you have some expertise."

"Yes, who are the characters in the story?" asked Dixie, expecting something outrageous.

He was not disappointed.

With a, this is going to be good grin, Mixie said, "It's about four big fat hairy assed rats!"

"Stop right there," spluttered Tilley, "you can't use language like that in a fairy tale," as she almost dropped her second, apple square.

"Uh oh, what have I said now?" asked Mixie. "No wait, I know, the word fat is forbidden, right?"

By this time in the conversation, Tilley had almost rolled off the grassy knoll, laughing. "No, no, it's not the word fat Mixie, it's the hairy assed bit."

Tilley was just about to make a further remark when Mixie held up her hand. "Shush, what was that?"

"Yes," said Dixie, "I heard a shout for help, I think."

With a puzzled look, Tilley said, "I didn't hear anything."

Quickly, as if in another world Mixie's persona changed, alert, in charge. "Along that track, Dixie." She pointed. "Wouldn't you say?"

He nodded. "Yeah, about two hundred metres, give or take."

"Yes, of course." Tilley instinctively touched the back pocket of her jeans.

"Okay," said Mixie. "You stay here. In the meantime, I'll give you a call if we need help, is that all right?"

Uncertainly, Tilley said, "Um, yes sure, what's happening?"

"There appears to be someone, a woman I would say needs help," Dixie explained.

Then the pixies were gone.

Moving quietly but quickly among the trees and ferns so as to remain relatively unseen the pixies soon found the source of the cry for help.

A woman lay on the track propping herself up on one elbow trying to examine her left leg.

"Hello," said Mixie quietly, "having a spot of trouble?"

"Damn, I think it's broken," said the jogger, wincing, then did a double take at the creature that had spoken to her, as she saw another come alongside the first. "Am I hallucinating or something?"

Mixie ignored the question and did a quick injury assessment... The woman was fit and strong...but best to keep her still.

"We are here to help," said Dixie. "Try not to move."

"What's your name?" asked Mixie.

"Uh, Susan, but...but...are you, what's going on?"

"My name is Mixie and this is Dixie, it looks like you have a compound fracture, the bone has broken through the skin, try not to move."

Dixie checked Susan's pulse, which was racing a bit.

"Bloody hell, it hurts like crazy, makes me want to squirm," said the grounded jogger.

Mixie pointed to the track. "That root was probably the culprit."

Looking at each other for a second or three, Dixie said, "St John could have problems getting a stretcher in here."

Looking through a gap in the bush towards the shore, Mixie said, "There's a flat bed of lava out there and the tides going out, what do you think?"

"Yep," he said, "while we stay with Susan, let's keep Tilley busy, see how she goes getting the Rescue Helicopter, et cetera, I'll go check out that lava."

"Okay," said Mixie, as she gave Tilley a buzz.

There was an instant reply, with Tilley saying, "What's up, what's the story?"

"We have a woman here, she tripped," said Mixie, "looks like a compound fracture, while we stay with her, could you get onto the police, ambulance and chopper, I'll give you the details."

"Uh, yes, um sure," came the reply from Tilley.

"Also," added Mixie, "walk to the tide line, look to your left, you'll see Dixie, that's where the helicopter needs to land."

"Okay," said Tilley, as she started the process, walked until the water was touching her toes, looked left, and there was a waving Dixie.

She wasn't sure why she felt relieved and reassured when she saw him, and just kept getting help.

***

The police arrived first, then the ambulance, all agreeing with Tilley the rescue would be easier by helicopter, with the pixies moving into the bush out of sight.

As all this was happening, Susan kept talking about two pixies, with a police officer remarking that she appeared to be in shock.

In due course when the kerfuffle was over and the crowd dispersed after cheering and shouting as the helicopter came thudding in and then out again, the three rescuers gathered again on their trusty knoll.

"Well, I don't know about you two, but that is my picnic over," said Tilley, "we'll try again another day, and maybe next time we'll see some fantails."

The pixies agreed as they all got in the car and made their way back to the embassy, but not until Tilley bought an ice cream at the local dairy.

Sitting outside the dairy enjoying her double crunchy Tilley suggested that Mixie finish telling them her fairy tale.

"Okay," she said, and did just that…

"Once upon a time, long, long, ago in another dimension four fat hairy assed rats lived in a rundown ramshackle seedy chateau; in which dwelt a lazy drunken old man and an even lazier cat.

"The main occupation of the dirty old man was boozing, eating and sleeping, and whilst the cat was teetotal it was even lazier and ate excessively more than its master.

"One day, the boss rat, the one with the red eyes suggested they play a practical joke on the cat, with the name of, Dork, as in big.

"The evil plan involved tying a soiled sweaty sock around the sleeping eyes of Dork and check out what happened when he was awakened by the clash of cymbals next to his left ear.

"Accordingly, during the absence of the lazy drunken O M the hairy bottomed rats put their diabolical plan to work.

"Ding! Bang! Clash!

"The cat woke with a start and shouted out that it couldn't see and immediately bumped into the edge of a door that was ajar (making it no longer a door) and started screaming for help.

"The door that was now a jar informed Dork help was not possible because of its change in status from a means of access and egress to now one of containment, while at the same time imploring the cat to have a nice day.

"With a scream of rage, the cat flung itself around the room, tripped over the cymbals, dislodged the sweaty sock and landed face first in its master's dinner which was waiting to be put in the oven.

"Now it so happened that steak and kidney pie was Big Dorks favourite activity which meant very little was left when the besotted old man arrived home thinking perhaps, he had devoured his meal in another life.

"It was at this stage that Dork settled down for a well-earned rest, followed by the old man, who went by the name of, Fred Nice, with the nick name of, Head Lice, falling face down upon a smelly bed where he lived happily ever after."

As they headed home the only comment made by Tilley was, "You'll never get that published."

Whilst at the same time, Dixie said, "I think the story was fantastic and reflects what life is all about the left hand doesn't know what the right foot is doing."

Parking the car, Tilley said, "I know what you little buggers were doing back there, it was a test how did I go?"

Mixie gave her that thousand-watt smile. "Well, for a PhD PA, not too bad at all, we'll keep you on."

The pixies raced for the elevator, followed by Tilley threatening torture, while at the same time feeling pretty good about her pass, but she couldn't work out why.

***

Last word from M & D: The difference between a fairy tale and reality is negligible, because right now we are having a lovely evening dancing on the head of a pin. No, we're not, only angels do that apparently.

Catch you later, have a spiffing day-old fruit, see yah! M & D.

Footnotes.

1. Parking exactly when one requires to is a common occurrence in Auckland, yeah right.

2. An imaginary knoll for the convenience of Tilley and the pixies.

The Muffin Man

Preface: Is there any creature more contrary than a human being? Well, pixies perhaps that happen to still be living in the lap of luxury at the embassy.
Author

***

Turning to the only other pixie on the balcony, he said, "I haven't seen Trixie or Vixie today."

Her look was thoughtful, as she murmured, "Didn't Trixie say something about going to Dunedin?"

Dixie thought about that possibility for a moment, before saying, "Why would she want to go to Dunedin?"

"That's right, now I remember," Mixie said, smiling at her most favourite pixie, "alcohol."

Their eyes met as he placed a bookmark in his latest tome 'Being Human Takes Time' as he said, "There's plenty of alcohol here besides that she doesn't drink."

"Illicit!" shouted Mixie, authoritatively.

He frowned. "What, Trixie is illicit?"

"No, no, Dixie, she's on some junket or other involving the illicit alcohol trade, it's all very mysterious and worldwide, apparently."

"Hmm" – he nodded – "that sounds pretty boring."

She gave an exaggerated and dramatic sigh. "Talking about boring, Dixie, I'm all for going out and about today, get rid of the embassy cobwebs."

"Where do you want to go?" he asked.

She hopped on the balcony safety rail pretending to walk a tightrope with her arms stuck out for balance. "How about we go to a shopping mall, there's nothing quite as entertaining as watching people dump money like there's no tomorrow."

He nodded. "Yeah, good idea and to make it more exciting we can be on the lookout for shoplifters and smokers."

Laughing, she said, "You mean, go out of our way to get into some sort of trouble."

He gave her the thumbs up, as she pretended to fall from the balcony rail with a shriek.

Peering over the rail, he saw her hovering, a metre from the ground. "Next time, try to fall on your head and knock some sense into it," he said, turning to run.

She chased him all the way to their room, threatening a fate worse than death.

"Which one?" he asked.

They were standing on the roof of the embassy, dressed in identical outfits, bright red polo shirts, black jeans and red patent leather shoes.

On the back of Mixie's shirt was, TOUCH ME AND DIE, while Dixie's read, GIVE IT A TRY.

"Well," she said, "for a start, how about, Meadow Ridge mall, it's close by."

"Okay, and if we can't get into enough trouble there we'll move on to, East Bank mall."

"Good plan," she said, as they drifted slowly over the roof tops an object buzzed past them.

Dixie grabbed at Mixie, saying, "Watch out, there goes a pizza delivery."

"Seen it," she said, with confidence, "damned nuisance those things."

He agreed, "Yeah, that's what people say about us, as well."

As the pixies moved across one property, a little boy pointed them out to his mother.

"Yes, dear," she said, "that must be those pesky life-like drones we have around here."

The dear little fellow smiled at his mother wanting to know more. "Do they work by battery, or are they wound up, mummy?"

Mixie glared at the nice little chap as he ran and held on to his mother's skirt, whimpering, "That nasty thing is looking at me, mummy, will it hurt us?"

As the mother picked her child up and clutched him to her bosom, she said, "No, sweetheart, they are programmed to be harmless."

Mixie stopped abruptly in mid-air. "I think I'll go down there, implant a battery in mummy and wind her up for good measure."

Shaking his head, Dixie said, "Just ignore her, we have better things to seek out and destroy at the mall."

"Yes, of course." She smiled, did a pirouette. "Let's go."

***

"Straight ahead," she said, pointing, as Meadow Ridge car park came into view.

As they got closer, Dixie stopped, looked at Mixie, as he did a slow-motion cartwheel, thoughtfully saying, "I've been thinking."

Mixie gave her beloved an ice melting smile. "Get it off your chest, sweetheart."

He stopped she did the same, as Dixie said, "How big is a portion do you think?"

She blinked, thought, "A portion of what?"

He shrugged. "Anything."

There was a long pause before she said, "Do you know, I think you have asked a question that would have interested, Albert, or maybe Stephen."

He nodded his agreement. "Yes, it's a bit like saying, be sure to eat five pieces of fruit per day."

"How so?" she asked, with a puzzled frown creasing her flawless brow.

Continuing on his way, he said over his shoulder, "How big is a piece?"

She caught up to him. "There's no doubt about you Dixie, you are a deep thinker, somewhat like a bottomless pit." She laughed, and did several somersaults, much to the delight of some dear old folk, alighting from a rest home bus.

In fact, some of the senior citizens almost fell off their walkers in excitement as they entered the mall arguing over which direction to take, with their minders trying to muster them to the planned route.

Entering the mall, Mixie stopped abruptly, saying, "Well, well, I'll be a monkey's uncle, look over there."

He looked, did a double take. "You could knock me down with feather," he said, "if I'm not mistaken, that is the guy who writes fairy tales."

And indeed, there stood, the author in the flesh, buying his weekly Lotto ticket, because he was no good at maths, or working out what thirty-eight million to one meant.

"He hasn't aged well," said Dixie.

She pulled a face. "Yeah, well, don't tell him that."

But Dixie was right...

There indeed was the author standing at the counter, about to throw away eighteen dollars...

Wisp of hair

Furrowed of brow

Droop of ear

Jaundiced of eye

Grim of mouth

Yellow of teeth

Dryness of lip

Crooked of body

Aching of bones

Tissue of skin

Flat feet and troubled of mind.

However, apart from all that his spirit was strong, and he was as fit as a buck rabbit with myxomatosis.

The troublemakers came alongside the weaver of dreams, with Mixie saying, "You're a long way from home oh ancient one, what's your excuse?"

Looking at the pixies with a kindly eye, the author said, "I saw you come in, somehow I knew you were going to be here, funny that."

"And you are here, because?" asked Dixie.

With a smile that hurt his jaws, the author said, "I am here to socialise."

A beat of silence passed before Mixie enquired, thoughtfully, "Socialise, with who, or is it whom?" Not knowing the difference, anyway.

The author raised his arms, did a turn, waving airily, before saying, "Everybody."

The pixies looked at each other for a fleeting moment, before saying, in unison, "You are too grumpy to talk to anybody."

Crinkling his eyes in a practised friendly manner, the author said, knowingly, "You don't necessarily have to talk to anyone to be sociable, ask any vicar."

"We talk all the time," said Dixie.

"You two," intoned the author, "prattle, nonstop, enough to give a donkey an earache."

The pixies beamed at the author, with Mixie saying, "We like talking and exchanging ideas, what was that question you asked me just now, Dixie?"

"Oh yeah, how big is a portion?"

"Ah." The author gave a sly smile, there was a twinkle in his eye. "You two can buy me a coffee and the biggest vanilla and boysenberry muffin you can find, that, my lovelies are how big a portion is."

Mixie's eyes went large and round, she folded her arms in a bossy manner. "It was a trap!" she shouted. "The author lured us into an ambush, Dixie."

"You're right, we should have known he was up to no good, you can't beat the author," acknowledged Dixie, with a bow.

"Get to it, shape up or ship out," growled the senior of all citizens, "time is a wasting."

With a sigh and shake of her head, Mixie said to her favourite pixie, "Got any money on you?"

He sighed. "Unfortunately yes, but where do we go for the biggest muffin in town?"

The author pointed, the pixies turned, a huge muffin sign smiled down on them.

"He's got it all worked out," she said, defeated, "come on, Dixie, let's pay the price, we may get a mention in one of his silly, long winded tales of woe."

The pixies wended their way to the MAX MUFFIN outlet with Dixie giving a smile to the smartly dressed attendant. "We want a massive vanilla and boysenberry muffin please, also a medium long black coffee, with hot water on the side."

"You have come to the right place," said the young woman, "we have muffins as big as all outdoors and the best coffee in town."

Mixie looked at the muffin woman through shrewd eyes her name tag identified her as, Shelly. "How big is big in your world?"

Shelly pointed with pride to the display under the glass counter, with the pixies doing a double take. "That's unbelievable," said Dixie, "they're almost as big as the author's head," which made Mixie smile.

"What is this going to cost?" asked the pixie paying the bill.

Shelly gave her best customer smile. "That will be, nineteen dollars and ninety-nine cents, thank you, sir."

Dixie peeled off a twenty-dollar bill. "Here you go, keep the change," as Mixie took the number for their table, which was, 12.5.

"What?" Dixie said.

"Ah yes" – Mixie gave a knowing nod – "humans think the number thirteen is unlucky."

As they sat down, with the self-satisfied author, Mixie said, "You are a decrepit old con man, a rip off merchant, and admit it, that was a well laid trap."

The author beamed at his little companions, as he struck a pose, saying, "Welcome death, quoth the rat, when the trap fell."

"Who said that?" asked Dixie.

Looking at the ceiling, stalling for time, the author finally said, "Um, I think it was some guy with the name of, Howell, back in the day."

"Never heard of him… What day," asked Mixie.

"Ah, here's my morning tea, which happens to be coffee," said the author, "uh, I think it was round about circa 1659, or thereabouts."

***

After warm farewells, because deep down the pixies had a fondness for the author the duo headed back to the embassy.

Flying backwards looking at her fellow dupe, Mixie said, "We fell for that ruse hook line and sinker."

"Yeah," agreed Dixie, as he pulled a face at the same little boy, sending him screaming to his mummy, "there's more to that old duffer than meets the eye."

As they entered the suite, Trixie appeared from her room. "Hi, you two, what have you been up to?"

A glance passed between the duo, as Mixie said, "We met the author and gave him a piece of our mind."

Looking at the duo, Trixie pursed her lips deep in thought, before saying, "How big is a piece, out of interest?"

Whispering through gritted teeth, Mixie said, "Don't you, start."

***

Postscript: A piece only becomes a portion in the eye of the beholder; when teeth gnash on the crust and the portion turns to dust.

The actual last word: How big is a particle and would half a dozen fill a thimble?

Just asking.

***

Home Sweet Home

Preface: Mid pleasures and palaces though we may roam
Be it ever so humble, there's no place like home.
John Howard Payne 1791–1852

***

In Tilley's car were, Mixie, Dixie and Marmalade, whilst the black security 'super bomb' contained Gil, Trixie and Vixie, making their way to the now completed, Pixie Villa, on an overcast and humid day.

The winding two hundred metre driveway had been completed in, asphalt, its black surface the better to blend with the surrounding bush and foliage.

As the cars rounded the last bend there stood the house as if it had been in situ for some time, unlike most new dwellings that usually stand out like a sore thumb.

Secondary bush, in the company of, kowhai, rata trees and ferns jostled for room, with a more cultured landscape up close and personal.

"Wow!" said Vixie. "I'll be able to do wonders with this place."

Trixie smiled, saying, "The good thing is, Dixie told me, all the plants and critters appear to be very talkative."

"Super!" said the only true lover of flora and fauna among the lot of them.

Gil smiled to himself as they all piled out of the two cars, holding back so that Mixie, Dixie and Marmalade could be first to enter the villa.

As they approached the house, Gil noted the two security guards had unobtrusively drifted to the rear of the property.

Having previously furnished the dwelling ready for the official opening, Mixie, Dixie and Marmalade skipped up the steps to the front door and keyed in the security code.

The cat, of course, was the first to enter, having pressed herself flat against the door.

"Come on, you lot," shouted Dixie, "last one in, is a rotten egg!"

Smiling, Gil happily trailed behind to be awarded the prize.

The villa was huge.

There would be a room for each pixie, when Trixie and Vixie stayed over.

A lounge completes with baby grand piano.

A dining room with standalone kitchen and walk in larder no less.

In the games room under the house was a self-contained flat.

Yes indeed…

Tilley and Gil stood back listening to the pixie chatter and merciless banter, but as things quietened down, Mixie said, "Tilley, Gil, would you like a cup of coffee?"

They both nodded, with Tilley saying, "Only if it's instant."

Mixie laughed. "You remind me of someone else which is another story she was a, businesswoman who claimed she loved instant coffee because it reminded her of her proud common roots."

"Anyway," Mixie continued, "the coffee is the only grocery in the larder, oh yes, and one more thing there, are some special biscuits in my duffle bag."

"Yeah, the only thing we forgot," said Dixie, "was the milk."

"Don't take milk," said Gil and Tilley at the same time, laughing at their 'double act'.

As Dixie went about manufacturing two cups of instant coffee, Mixie placed the biscuits on a side table.

Gil looked closely…

As Tilley raised an eyebrow…

With her saying, "They're green."

"But a very nice green," Gil added.

A knowing look passed between the pixies, before Mixie said, "I baked them early this morning at the embassy, try one."

Tilley ventured to take a bite, chewed slowly, swallowed, looked at Mixie, saying, "This biscuit is absolutely delicious, how did you make that happen?"

As he munched, Gil nodded. "Yes, amazing… Why are they green?"

Mixie beamed with delight. "Because the basis of that particular biscuit happens to be, gooseberries, with natural fruit juice as a sweetener."

"No sugar?" asked Tilley.

"No sugar," confirmed, Mixie.

Gil who knew very little about cooking, other than baked beans and Tilley who knew even less remained silent, trying to catch up.

Eventually breaking the silence, Trixie said, "Years ago, Mixie and Dixie ran a small business where they made and sold biscuits."

"And I did the selling," said Vixie.

Very slowly, Tilley said to Vixie, "You sold biscuits, I find that hard to imagine."

"I can be a very persuasive salesperson," said Vixie, with her most innocent smile.

"Now that I can believe," said Tilley, making everyone laugh, even Vixie.

The following silence was broken by Mixie saying, "One of these days we'll explain our escapades in another sort of world, but for now, let's see what we can see from the back of the house sundeck."

They found Marmalade stretched out on the deck as if she owned the place, already (she did).

Opening one eye, the cat thought… *How long will it take for M & D to get into trouble of some sort?* Then relaxed until that inevitable moment in time.

The party of six looked out over the surrounding landscape, with Tilley saying, "You are fortunate to still have a lot of natural bushes and the ferns are just gorgeous…lovely."

Gil pointed to his right. "It looks like your nearest neighbour is about two hundred metres or so, and even then, there is only part of their roof showing."

"Yes, a lot of this area is a reserve, so there won't be too many more dwellings around here," said Trixie.

The group chatted, reminisced, relaxed, the afternoon drifted to evening, as Gil stood saying, "Well, you guys, I have to love and leave you, work beckons."

"So, Gil, before you go, what's the story with the security guys," asked Vixie.

"Yeah," he said, "the story with them is we'll keep security here for a few weeks, just to make sure all is normal, especially if the villa is left empty."

"And," continued Trixie, "should, M & D be away for any length of time."

"Okay," said Gil, "I'm on my way, oh, how are you guys for transport?"

Trixie gave a laugh. "We are all staying overnight to annoy, Mixie and Dixie transport will be no problem."

"Right," said Gil, and was on his way.

A relaxed silence settled over the group, with Marmalade forced to open an eye to check all was well, it was.

Then an excited, "Look at that," came from Mixie as she pointed towards the far end of the sundeck.

All heads turned including a now wide awake, Marmalade.

There, sitting on the deck rail were two fantails.

A tear rolled down Mixie's cheek, as she said, "That's a good omen, right?"

"It is indeed," said Tilley, as the birds took off up and over the roof, "wonderful."

There was a quietness once again, until Vixie said, looking at M & D, "How about you two giving us a tune or six on this very special occasion."

Tilley was left wondering what else the pixies were capable of doing.

Dixie looked at his most favourite pixie, who nodded.

Wandering to the lounge, they arranged themselves around the baby grand, including, Marmalade.

Dixie ran his fingers over the keys as he and Mixie had a bit of a chat about what to play, before he said, "We have decided to play a few melodies from the past."

"Plus," MIxie said, smiling, "a few more recent numbers."

They sat side by side, with Tilley completely blown away at what followed.

At the end, there wasn't a dry eye in the house, except for Marmalade who had fallen asleep.

That evening, when Tilley went to the village to purchase groceries the pixies were relaxing, thinking their own thoughts, when Vixie said quietly, "I'm so happy about what's happened."

They had a quadruple hug and shed a tear or two for old times and memories.

***

The next morning, sitting at the dining room table, Tilley said, "Do you all have to watch me eat my breakfast?"

"Yes, of course," said Mixie, "as part of the family you will now be continually and constantly annoyed by ever present pixies, right Marmalade."

From under the table was a tangible silence, with the cat thinking – tell me about it.

"Anyway," said Trixie ominously, "now that we are all here there is something I would like to discuss."

"Uh oh, what bombshell is about to explode?" asked Dixie, uneasily.

Under the table, Marmalade thought… *I was right here we go again. The, you know what is about to hit the fan.*

Ignoring Dixie's question, but answering it at the same time, Trixie said, "As you know Vixie and I are still involved in the pesky alcohol saga, that won't go away." She shrugged, raising her eyebrows.

With a turned down mouth, Dixie said, "You will find, Tilley, when Trixie shrugs there is some form of catastrophe looming."

"It's not trouble, just another adventure," said Vixie.

With a hard stare at Trixie, Mixie said, "Well, come on spill your guts."

"Okay," said Trixie, staring back. "What does the name Gene mean to you?"

"Oh no!" said Dixie, vehemently, "sand in my underwear is what it would mean."

Tilley nearly choked on her cornflakes, never having witnessed a pixie breakfast meeting before.

"Yes," said Mixie, her eyes sparking, "and the aromas out there are not great either."

"Jeez, this is fantastic," said Tilley, "it's the best breakfast meeting I have ever attended, and I've been to plenty."

With Vixie saying, "It's not funny, Tilley."

"Yes, it is," said the PA gulping down her coffee and regretting it as she had a coughing fit.

As all the pixies hit Tilley on the back, she thought, am I going to regret this?

As a relative calm descended over the group, Trixie said, "Getting back to the point, there is an important diplomatic assignment in, Baghdad."

Tilley suddenly became very alert, with yet another thought, this is for real.

With slit eyes and pursed lips, Mixie said, "Give us the gritty info, Trixie."

"Um, Gene is having trouble with that cousin of his, again," said the multi-millionaire.

"I don't believe it," said Dixie, "not that no hoper, Aladdin, what's he done this time?"

"Yes, and why can't the Iraq pixies or whatever they call them over their deal with it?" growled Mixie.

Shaking her head in frustration, Trixie said, "Their mythological fraternity are flat out dealing with all the aftermath of the crazy wars and skirmishes and need our help, it came through the embassy."

"Oh," said M & D in unison, and feeling somewhat admonished.

"Excuse me please, just a minute," said Tilley, "are you talking about that Aladdin guy with the magic lamp thingy."

The pixies fell about laughing, with Trixie saying, "No, no, that is just a silly myth, a children's story, the Aladdin we are talking about is a cleaner, a real person."

"Who's, speciality happens to be in restoring old lamps," added Vixie.

With a sigh, Tilley felt obliged to get more information. "You say that you have dealt with this Aladdin person before, in what way?"

Four pairs of pixie eyes met, with Mixie saying as she looked at Trixie, "Are we allowed to say the word without fear of court action?"

"Uh um," mumbled Trixie uncertainly, "only within these four walls and you Tilley will never mention this conversation to anyone."

"Right, I understand," said the PA, "I think."

"Dixie and I several years ago paid a visit to Baghdad under similar circumstances, our assignment being to help Aladdin to lose, um, weight," said Mixie lowering her voice.

"You mean he was fat!" said Tilley, loudly and forthrightly.

The pixies were aghast, Marmalade too, with Vixie saying, "Be very careful where you use the F word, Tilley."

"Yes," said Dixie, "we were left in no doubt that the F word was not to be used."

"Ah, I get it," said Tilley, "political correctness, yes, very important, because of feelings and so on, so what did you use instead of the F word?"

"Big boned," said Mixie, drily.

No one laughed out of respect for the larger person.

With a frown, Tilley said, "What's the problem this time?"

All eyes turned to Trixie, even Marmalade came out from under the table.

"Ah," said Trixie weakly, trying to smile, "same thing, I understand."

With a frustrated look at Mixie, her other half said, "After all the effort we put in the, um, large one has done it again."

"Put him down," I say, growled Vixie.

All present considered Vixie's reasonable suggestion, with Trixie saying finally, "Yeah, tempting, but unfortunately this never-ending saga has reached diplomatic level."

"Who has got the pull to get this mess that far?" asked Vixie.

M & D's eyes met, with Mixie saying, "We think Gene has a dodgy relative in government."

The awkward silence was broken by Trixie coughing discreetly before she said, "Uh, there is one other thing." Her smile was not its usual confident self.

All eyes settled on the government/private sector employee.

"Yes, well, because of its diplomatic status, I would have normally accompanied Mixie and Dixie," explained Trixie, "but because of other work, it will need to be another embassy member."

This time, all eyes, settled on Tilley. Who smiled, followed quickly by a look of alarm. "Me, I don't like creepy crawlies or heat."

"You'll soon get used to it," said Mixie, quietly, kindly but assertively.

"Yes also, you will get full embassy backing a six-star hotel and a car to run around in, or a chauffeur if you like," added Trixie.

"Plus, the adventure and excitement of working with Mixie and Dixie, with a few cock ups thrown in for good measure that's for sure," said Vixie, without smiling.

"I'll do it," said Tilley, quietly but confidently. All cheered, with Marmalade thinking… *Only the naïve are brave, or foolhardy…*

"The other thing being, you will be going by embassy plane," the confident smile was, now back on Trixie's face.

"By the way, Tilley, what's this PhD thingy all about?" asked Dixie.

"I'll give it to you in one word," said the PA, "finance."

Trixie smiled. "Tilley is a financial genius, that's why I hired her."

"Hmm," said Dixie, "that expertise combined with her unarmed combat skills maybe useful in the land of grit."

***

Postscript: To travel hopefully is a better thing than to arrive, and the true success is to labour. Robert Louis Stevenson, 13 Nov. 1850–3 Dec. 1894. Pixies are forever hopeful, with Tilley hoping she will come out the other end unharmed.

***

Kismet

Preface: Five hours sleepeth a traveller, seven a scholar, eight a merchant, eleven every knave, none a pixie.

Proverb (adapted) authorship unknown

Tilley always slept for seven hours, whether she travelled or not you could set your clock by her, funny that.

Author

***

A resigned to his fate Dixie said to his work colleagues, "Well, we best be getting organised for our Middle East trip."

"Yep," agreed Mixie, with a sigh, "but at least we have the luxury of travelling by embassy plane."

Whereas, a still stunned Tilley was coming to terms with her travel plans to an unknown fate, as she said, "So what do we need to organise by way of luggage?"

There came a thoughtful, "Hmm," from Mixie, followed by, "something lightweight and in my opinion covering our legs because of the biting thingy's out there."

Yet another pang of anxiety stabbed at Tilley's stomach.

"Right, decision made," said Dixie, "pixie combat outfit for me."

Mixie nodded her agreement. "Yes that would be perfect."

The one-piece garment Dixie referred to was of irradiance lightweight fine mesh, coloured red, green and khaki.

Looking at a befuddled Tilley, Mixie said, "Any ideas as to your wardrobe?"

"Um," came from the having second thoughts PA.

"May I suggest," said Mixie, cheerfully, "pack anything that is lighter than a feather is drip dry cotton, with trousers at all times and some hats."

Tilley nodded. "Okay, but I'll need to do some shopping."

Dixie gave her his helpful smile. "That's okay we can come with you all expenses on the embassy, right Mixie?"

"Right!" said the effervescent female pixie, as yet another stab of the gut churning angst struck at Tilley's nether region, imagining a shopping trip with two chatty and advising partners.

***

As the three cohorts were boarding the plane, a sweet little girl in a pretty lemon dress said, "Daddy, can I press the buttons on those two robots and make them jiggle?"

Mixie gave the sweetheart child a look that sent her screaming into her father's arms, who said, "They're not robots darling, but very realistic androids, you only have to look at their artificial flawless skin to tell that."

The same look and a whisper sent daddy hurrying to the toilet to check if all was well...

During the flight, everything went swimmingly, with the only major incident being the little girl ran rampant throughout the plane and managed to spill orange juice over the business suit of an Under Secretary.

The father was oblivious to the actions of his daughter as he played continuously with his yoyo.

Without further ado, Mixie took the child to one side and whispered in her ear.

From then on, the little girl sat quietly reading, 'The Rise and fall of the Roman Empire'.

Oh yes, it just so happened that Tilley missed all the excitement because of her seven-hour sleeping period. "I didn't hear a thing," she said, as the plane landed.

Some people could sleep on a bed of nails.

***

The trio were duly picked up at the airport by a chauffeur with the name of, Cuthbert, driving a limo.

"I notice a bit of an accent, Cuthbert," said Tilley, "where are you from?"

"Me, miss, my home base is, Acne," he said.

"I didn't know a place could be named after a pimple," whispered Dixie.

Tilley smiled. "It's Hackney, right Cuthbert?"

"That's right," he said, "Acne, and you can call me, Bert."

The name of their hotel was, 'Paradiso', and certainly deserved its six-star rating.

Wandering into Mixie's room, Tilley said, "Where are you?"

"In one of the showers," shouted Mixie.

Just then, Dixie walked in, saying, "There are two bathrooms his and hers."

Coming out of the bathroom in a robe with a towel wrapped around her hair, Tilley's first thought was, *How sweet, she could be a tiny human*, but didn't say anything.

"So, what's the plan?" asked the financial genius.

Before Mixie could say anything, her off-sider asked politely, "First, I want to know what you said to that horrible child to shut her up."

With an innocent smile, Mixie said, "I lied and told her if she was a good girl, she could push your buttons when the plane landed."

"What!" he said, as Tilley flung herself on the bed laughing.

"Fortunately, we got caught up in the kerfuffle of the airport, Dixie, or you may have had that little bugger poking you in all sorts of places," said the only female pixie in the room.

Tilley couldn't stop laughing as she gasped. "You two should be on the stage."

"Hmm," he said, narrow eyeing Mixie, "I'll get you later. By the way, Tilley, how's your Arabic?"

Quickly returning to business of the day, Tilley said, "South of nil," with a shrug.

"We can get by," said Mixie, "but a lot of people speak English here, anyway."

Tilley nodded. "Okay." She looked at her mobile, scrolling, "I see that in town, the temperature is thirty-eight Celsius, feels like forty-one."

"Yeah," came from Dixie, "and where we are going, there is no air conditioning."

"Speaking of that," said Mixie, "we need to get more facts, so as to form a plan, our next move will be to visit Aladdin at 13 Caliph Lane." She looked at Dixie.

He nodded his agreement. "Yes, and that part of town is a fair way from here, we need to talk to, Bert."

Within five minutes, Bert who had been waiting for the call was sitting in the room, saying, "Caliph Lane, you sure know how to pick 'em."

"Yes," said Mixie with a sigh, "not a very classy part of town, to say the least, number thirteen."

"Ah yeah, I won't be able to park, but I'll keep driving around, so I'm on call pretty quickly," said Bert.

***

As the car entered Caliph Lane, even with the windows shut and air conditioning flat out, Tilley said, "What's that smell?"

Mixie pointed as Dixie said, "That ditch is an open sewer."

With Bert adding, "Where they dump all their, um, stuff."

"What have I got myself into?" asked Tilley, quietly to herself.

"Hopefully, not that ditch," said a smiling Mixie.

Getting out of the car, Dixie said, as Bert drove away, "Try not to hold your breath, Tilley, because the next time you inhale, you'll fall over."

Few people looked at the slightly unusual group being used to the weird in this part of town, as they approached number thirteen.

"Do we knock?" asked Tilley.

"No way," said Mixie, "the element of surprise is paramount."

"The door will be locked, surely," Tilley found herself whispering.

Dixie had moved ahead and was already at the door, with Mixie saying, "The best picklock in the world has already worked his magic," as the door swung open.

Tilley just shook her head.

Once inside, Dixie closed the door and quietly relocked it.

Tilley twitched her nose. "The nasty smell has faded a bit, but now there's another."

"That aroma will be the spices Aladdin uses for his gargantuan meals," explained Mixie.

"So where is he?" asked Tilley.

Dixie nodded towards a flight of stairs. "He lives in a dingy garret, walk to the extreme left or right that helps to avoid creaking."

The new secret agent slotted that useful piece of information away for future use.

As they made their way up the stairs, music could be heard. "That'll be the TV, he usually watches old DVD's, anything about fairy land," said Mixie.

"Yeah," growled Dixie, "he's a very unrealistic person, always daydreaming."

As they got to a small landing, Mixie said to her partner, "Are you going to be the good cop or bad cop this time?"

He whispered, "I suggest we stick to this routine, I'll be the good cop, you Tilley, stand quietly behind Aladdin for later."

Why later? Was the thought that entered Tilley's mind.

As they quietly entered a dingy room, there was Aladdin overflowing in a chair with his eyes fixed on the TV screen, in a hypnotic trance.

Moving slowly between the rabid viewer and the screen, M & D waited.

It took a few minutes before Aladdin responded, his tone was peevish, "Who are you?" Upon getting no response, he grumbled, "More to the point, what are you, pizza delivery?"

"Don't you recognise us, Aladdin," said Dixie, "we are here to help you. again!"

Frowning deeply, the Baghdad resident mumbled unsurely, "Why would I need help?"

A pixie second flicked by…

Then with sudden recognition, Aladdin blurted, "Oh no, not you two troublemakers!"

"Ah yes," purred Mixie, giving the larger-than-life fellow the full benefit of her hypnotic eyes, "you remember us." Another pause.

"Listen up," she continued, "your mythological community are tied up with other stuff so it's going to be more of the same, Aladdin, do I make myself clear?"

"Ah," was Aladdin's weak but thoughtful reply.

"Aladdin," said Dixie, in a kindly good cop tone, "you are obviously aware of your morbid condition, what we would like to know is how such an unfortunate state came about, once again?"

At which stage, M & D went completely silent and still.

While all the while Tilley looked, listened and learned…

Aladdin sank deeper in his groaning chair, before saying quietly, with a faraway look in his eyes. "Powerball."

A puzzled look passed between the good and bad cop, before Mixie said, "Powerball, the game of chance, am I right?"

"You certainly are, and it was a bad chance for me," said Aladdin, with a shrug.

Dixie waited a tick or two, before saying, "A bad chance for you, Aladdin, how so?"

A long silence ensued, where M & D bit their respective tongues and cherished a silence that can often bring forth precious human insights.

Still looking past, the duo, Aladdin said simply, "My fiancé, Sharaz, won Powerball when overseas and ran off with a money grabbing playboy."

If it wasn't so sad, it would be funny, thought Dixie.

If it wasn't so funny, it would sad, thought Mixie.

While Tilley thought, *Good on her…*

With an encouraging smile, Dixie said, "This was when, Aladdin?"

"Uh, let me see," the beefy Iraq citizen scratched his head, shedding dandruff, "about a year ago."

Mixie nodded thoughtfully, giving her partner a wink, "Aladdin's condition, if I'm not mistaken is known as, 'slough of despond syndrome', what do you think?"

Giving an insightful squint, Dixie intoned, "Yes, known to the medical profession as SODS."

Alarmed, panic in his voice, Aladdin blurted, "Sods! I've got sods? Is it…terminal…contagious?"

"Calm down, Aladdin, that is why we are here," cooed Dixie.

Coming back into the conversation, the, bad cop, said, "Yes, your good friend, Gene, has become sick with worry, how do you feel about that?"

"Tell me what I have to do, just give it to me straight," said a very guilty feeling, Aladdin.

Looking at the man sitting in the dilapidated adjustable chair, Mixie growled, "You have to lose half your body weight, buster, simple as that, join a gym or something."

The terrible two eased off at this stage waiting to see which way Aladdin would choose to jump.

Aladdin was silent for a long moment, then dislodging himself from his comfort zone waddled to a two-door cupboard and flung it open. "I've still got all my exercise equipment from last time."

Keeping the pressure on, Mixie snarled. "Nothing like starting right now."

"Yes," said Dixie, in a kindlier tone, "but ease into it, and by the way, does Gene still live out back in the marquee?"

Aladdin nodded. "Yes, he's still there, we haven't sold the land yet."

"Before we go, meet our other team member, Tilley, she is a government agent," said Mixie.

"Hello, Aladdin, pleased to meet you," she said, coming around to shake him by the hand.

Startled, Aladdin said, "Have you been there all the time?"

"I have indeed," said Tilley, "and there is something I noticed earlier, when that princess came on screen, you perked up, ran your fingers through your hair, what does that tell us?"

"Um," said Aladdin shyly, "I like princesses."

"Yes, indeed," said the newly promoted PA.

***

As the trio made their way to the marquee, Mixie said to Tilley, "Well spotted, all we need now is a princess to add a bit of motivation."

Tilley couldn't work out why she felt good about being praised by a pixie.

"How would you rate my snarl, this time, Dixie?" asked his partner.

"Huge improvement," he said, "huge but I think you could inject even more venom, with practice."

She nodded. "I'll work on it."

Laughing out loud, Tilley said, "You two are the best double act I've ever seen."

Giving Dixie a squeeze, which left him breathless, Mixie said, thoughtfully, "Yes, Tilley, we have had many years of practice."

"Right," said Dixie, equally as thoughtful, "practice is good, but only if you practice the right things."

Leaving Tilley very thoughtful…

As they approached the marquee, a booming voice echoed off the surrounding buildings. "Hello, Mixie haven't seen you in a long while."

"Hi, big boy," said Mixie as they entered the large tent, "I've got company."

They came upon a scene which was poignant, a large, no, enormous figure sitting Buddha-like on a platform, above which was a shade-less two-hundred-watt power guzzling bulb.

Gene's sad eyes welcomed his visitors as Mixie whispered, "He's not well, we got here just in time, I hope."

"I heard that," said Gene, trying to force a smile.

"You were meant to, my friend," she said.

"So, we have a pair of pixies and a beautiful young woman," said Gene, "I'm so relieved to see you, I was becoming very distressed."

Tilley couldn't work out why she felt strangely buoyant.

"I now think," added Gene, "that the situation is in safe hands."

All four fell silent for several thoughtful moments, before Mixie said, "You know, it appears to me Gene that you are suffering from a severe case of empathetic transfer."

His eyes popping with alarm, Gene said, "Is that anything like the measles?"

"No," explained Mixie, "you have feelings for Aladdin much like a father-to-be has phantom sympathy pains on behalf of his partner."

"Yes indeed," said Dixie, "as Aladdin gets his act together, so too will you become well again."

Smiling, Gene said, "As a matter of fact, I'm already beginning to feel an improvement."

"Good, because we have Aladdin on a fitness regime, as we speak," announced, Mixie.

Tilley moved forward a fraction, before saying, "Tell us about the Powerball fiasco."

"Hmm, yes," Gene nodded, "if it hadn't been so sad, it would have been funny."

His three visitors controlled their reactions.

"How much did Sharaz win, out of interest?" asked the financial genius.

"Millions and millions," explained Gene, "she was overseas at the time working as a nurse."

"Anyway," said Mixie, snapping back to the task at hand, "a question, Gene, where can we find a princess around here?"

Looking at Mixie with hooded eyes, Gene said, "Princesses do not grow on trees, they are very hard to come by in this part of town."

"What I really mean, Gene, is a metaphorical princess," explained Mixie.

"Oh, I see," said Gene, one of those, "a make-believe princess."

With a sigh, Mixie decided to come clean. "Look, not real royalty, of course, but Aladdin comes alive when he catches a glimpse of a princess on television."

"Yeah," added Dixie, "Tilley spotted it, it could make all the difference to Aladdin's recovery."

"Right," said Gene, "and the sooner Aladdin comes right, the sooner yours truly returns to his devilish best, um, I do have a suggestion."

"Ah," said the trio, in unison.

"The Magic Bazaar, specifically, the southern end," said Gene, then promptly went to sleep, sitting upright.

The blank looks on three faces indicated further explanation was required.

A tick of pixie silence took place.

"He needs his rest, leave him for now," said Mixie, "it's getting late we'll visit this, Magic Bazaar tomorrow early and check it out."

As they left the marquee, the sleeping Gene, said wisely, "Hmm."

The three just kept going, checking in on Aladdin, who they found cycling flat out to nowhere in particular, as Tilley gave Bert a buzz.

The car (including Bert) was at the door before they could say, Jack Robinson.

As the trio was transported back to the hotel, several actions were agreed upon, including:

Concentration was now squarely on getting Aladdin fit and well again.

The exercise equipment would be moved to the marquee in order for Aladdin and Gene to support each other.

A dietary programme to be instigated based upon the book, 'Eating Less for More' with strict refrigerator rules enforced.

During the last five minutes of the journey to the hotel, Tilley fell into a sound sleep which was very unlike her.

As they got out of the car, Bert said, "Remember, I'm available twenty-four seven."

"Do you know, Gil?" asked, Tilley, sleepily.

Bert just smiled and drove away.

***

Sitting on Mixie's bed, Tilley said, "I'm going to turn in early tonight, but first there are some questions that I know I'll regret asking."

The pixies looked at each other, smiled, with Dixie saying, "Of course you will."

Taking a deep breath and leaning back on three fluffy pillows, Tilley said, "You guys have been through this exercise before, right?"

She then slept soundly for seven hours…

As the pixies covered her with a blanket, Mixie said, "Perhaps we'll tell her our story one day."

***

The next day M, D and T explored the surrounding district with Bert taking them to the, Magic Bazaar.

Entering the northern end of the bazaar, the stalls, small shops and street vendors were of a high quality, colourful and expensive, whereas, a gradual deterioration took place as they wandered further south.

They mingled, poked at stuff, tried on hats and bought nothing, until Tilley said, "Look at this silk scarf, Mixie, it's the exact colour of your eyes, try it on."

"I don't usually wear stuff like that," said the only female pixie from the southern hemisphere in the bazaar.

"Go on, give it a go," encouraged Dixie.

She wound the scarf around her neck with Tilley arranging it properly, as Dixie said, "Wow, I could fall for you all over again."

The tough pixie warrior blushed as Tilley bought the scarf on the spot.

As they wandered, Dixie especially, was fascinated by the street games, tricks and so-called magic acts.

Making their way further south the pixies were surprised to see a 'Shell Game' underway.

"That's unusual for this part of the world," said Dixie, "it's an oldie but a goody."

"True," Mixie agreed, "but the poor saps are unaware that there is no pea under any of the shells when they come to choose."

"Then boom! They lose their money, it's the quickness of the hand deceiving the eye," he said, adding, "at the same time quite clever."

The trio continued to move south and smelt it before they saw it.

There was an odour not thoroughly unpleasant but pungent with a variety of spices and the odd whiff from an open sewer thrown in for good measure.

The stalls were ramshackle, run-down lean-to wood and canvas buildings, with plenty of on-the-ground produce, colourful, but reflected the area, in a word, poor.

Abruptly, Tilley stopped, the pixies gawking elsewhere bumping into her, "Over there, what do you make of that young woman?" she whispered, pointing.

"Hmm," said both pixies.

"Yes," said Tilley, thoughtfully, "ignore everything else accept her face and demeanour, what is your first impression?"

Mixie said, "Well, first foremost, and most important, I see a woman trying to maintain her dignity against all odds."

"Yeah, I agree," said Dixie, "it can't be easy for her, look at the appalling work conditions. There must be an evil owner in the background, and what is that terrible gunk she's selling?"

Weighing up the situation, Tilley said, "We'll wait for a lull in trade, then go and ask her."

"That sounds like a plan," said Mixie.

A few minutes later, they approached the stall and all three noticed something at the same time. "She has a brutal looking bruise on her left cheek," said Mixie, her voice hardening.

"We need to play it cool," said Dixie, "is it a result of a work accident or something more sinister?"

"Hello," said Mixie, pleasantly, "how are you today?"

The woman looked up in surprise. "Ah," she said and proceeded to talk in English with a fascinating accent. "I noticed you three just now, that is a lovely scarf it blends perfectly with your amazingly beautiful eyes."

"Thank you, so much," said Mixie, "how are things going with you?"

"Um, very well," said the young woman.

"My name is Tilley, and these are my friends, Mixie and Dixie, what is your name?" asked the ex-PA.

"Kismet," said the stall minder proudly.

There was an intake of breath from Mixie. "Fate or destiny, is that right?"

Kismet smiled. "Sort of."

"We are interested in your, uh, just what is it you sell, Kismet?" asked Dixie.

"This is a weed from the rivers Tigris and Euphrates, cooked, dried and smoked, it's what poor people eat," explained Kismet.

"That could be quite nourishing," said Tilley, "where do you live, Kismet?"

She nodded towards the back of the lean-to. "Behind that curtain."

Silence settled over the group as they grappled with the thought of living and sleeping in such a place.

"No family close by?" enquired Mixie, trying to be diplomatic.

A beat or two of silence before Kismet said, "They were all killed in the war I'm the only one left."

"We are so sorry," said Mixie, touching Kismet's hand, "how horrible for you."

Kismet stood resolute, all her crying long over. "Thank you," she said, simply.

Always the opportunist, Dixie said, "You seem to have been in the wars yourself," pointing to Kismet's bruise.

The food vendor became visibly uneasy and stuttered, "Um, uh, I bumped into the edge of a door it's nothing."

Sensing an opening in the conversation, Mixie asked casually, "Who's your employer, Kismet?"

"Oh," she was visibly startled by the question, "um, a Mr Farouk, he owns this stall and many other things in the city."

Unseen by the others, a smile flickered across Tilley's face.

Dixie's question was kindly put, but blunt and to the point. "He hit you, didn't he?"

With panic in her eyes, Kismet blurted, "I have nothing to say, this is the only job I could get and somewhere to sleep, you must leave now."

"Yes, yes, we are leaving, just one question, Kismet," asked Mixie, "when is your employer here next?"

"Uh, probably tomorrow afternoon, now please leave," said Kismet, with some agitation in her voice.

As they made their way out of the bazaar, Mixie hissed, "We are going to get that bastard, right?"

"In one way or another," said Tilley quietly, "the goodies, which are us, always win in the end."

Mixie shook her head in frustration. "We'll talk it over. I can see now why Gene wanted us to visit the bazaar. I won't sleep tonight."

"Pixies never sleep, anyway," said Dixie.

Shaking her head, Mixie said, "I know, but I won't rest 'til Farouk is dealt with, in the nastiest possible way."

"We need to hit him in the wallet," said Tilley quietly, "not the balls."

"Let's do both," whispered Mixie, with malice aforethought.

They exited the bazaar with Bert ready to go.

As they were heading for Caliph Lane, Tilley said, "Bert, where can I get access to state of the art computer stuff?"

"Well, it won't be at the hotel," he said, "but probably at the embassy, leave it with me, I'll give you a buzz after dropping you off."

"Good," said Tilley, "I need to get at someone's algorithms."

Mixie eyeballed her off-sider. "Them little buggers, remember we had trouble with those critters some time ago?"

"Yeah," he said, "they need putting down."

"Also," said Tilley, "his assets will be frozen."

"That could be painful," said Dixie.

The pixies' eyes met. "There won't be much left of Mister F when Tilley's finished with him," chortled Mixie.

Back at Caliph Lane, as they entered the marquee, Dixie said, looking at Aladdin trembling like a jelly on a vibration contraption, "He's shaping up nicely and appears to be very dedicated."

"Hmm," said Mixie, preoccupied, "the flab has diminished but he may have to go under the knife for his flaps."

"You missed your vocation, Mixie, you should have been a surgeon," said Dixie, but she wasn't listening.

"Greetings, my lovelies," said Gene, "you have been talking to Kismet, I can tell."

"He's almost back to full strength," whispered Mixie, happily.

"I heard that," said the big guy.

Mixie laughed. "You were meant to."

Indeed, Gene had become svelte-like, with an aura of latent power about him. "What did you learn," he asked, "upon your visit to the bazaar?"

"Let me sum up the situation this way," said Mixie, "we didn't like what she told us, what she didn't tell us, or what we saw."

Between them, the trio related their encounter with Kismet, as Gene acknowledged the problem had worsened.

It was at that stage a call came through for Tilley, with Bert informing her that an embassy computer was available as and when required.

"Excellent," said the destroyer of Swiss Bank accounts, "can you pick us up in about ten minutes, Bert, right, and thank you very much."

"That Bert is something else," said Mixie.

Tilley smiled knowingly. "There is more to Bert, than any of us is going to find out."

"What we need now is information about the infamous Mr F, what can you tell us about him, Gene?" said Dixie.

"Yeah, well," Gene said, thoughtfully, "let me see, he owns stalls at both ends of the market, at least a dozen high end restaurants, bribes officials, evades taxes; has a wife and several other friends, if you know what I mean, and so on."

"Ah," murmured Tilley, more to herself than anyone else, "I think we have him now by the short and curly."

"Ouch!" said Gene, as they all fell about laughing.

"What does he look like?" asked Mixie.

Again, Gene gave the question some thought, before saying, "He's spherical in silhouette and soaks up food like a sponge absorbs water."

"You mean he's F," said Dixie, uneasily, looking over his shoulder.

Gene's eyes popped. "Are we allowed to use that word?" he whispered.

"Only when the mind police are washing their smalls," said Mixie, sadly.

Tilley smiled at the group, as Aladdin gasped falling off his machine in a glutinous heap. "Our plan will be cunning, which is much better than an ordinary plan, because it contains vindictiveness, I just love this job of being a secret agent."

***

The vindictive plan was formed and implemented. Tilley performed her magic at the embassy and the group of four which now included Aladdin arrived at the bazaar, where they mixed and mingled close to Kismet's workplace.

Then, sure enough, just after noon a blimp of a man puffed up with his own self-importance pushed his way unceremoniously through the crowd, accompanied by a large muscular minder, as anticipated by the conspirators.

Upon his arrival, Mr Farouk immediately began to berate a cowering Kismet, his words lost in the general hubbub of the crowd.

Dixie restrained his partner, reminding her of their plan, whereby Mixie got alongside the minder and said, "Hi, I bet you're an important part of Mr Farouk's staff."

Distracted by the cute pixie, the beefy one became preoccupied and wouldn't shut up about how important he was.

In the meantime, Aladdin hovered in the background ready to whisk Kismet to safety.

What of Tilley and Dixie?

Well, Tilley confronted the stall owner, saying, "Good afternoon, Mr Farouk, oh boy have I got a deal for you."

"What?" said the perplexed despot, as he stopped mid-berate, his beady, snake-like eyes fixed on the financial genius.

"Yes, indeed and here's the deal, Mr Farouk," she said, as Dixie landed on his left shoulder and gripped his ear as only a pixie can.

"I'll come straight to the point," said Tilley, as Dixie easily dodged the grabbing hands of Farouk and went for the other ear.

"The deal is you have to treat your staff properly, or certain things could happen," said Tilley.

"Or what," snarled Farouk.

To be fair, Dixie did admire the snarl, which was the best he had ever heard.

With an easy-going smile and a twinkle in her eye, Tilley said, "Or the money will disappear from your Swiss Bank Accounts, plus your cronies will desert you."

A quieter more thoughtful Farouk said, still trying to grab at Dixie, "That is impossible."

Tilley's manner was calm as she contacted Gene at the embassy. "Hi, patch us in to Mr F's Swiss bank manager, thanks."

"As we speak." Gene chuckled, enjoying the thrill of the chase.

It was at that moment, the beefy minder noticed all was not well with his master and began to move, whereby Mixie simply got under his feet tripping him into the crowd, who took out their frustrations on the poor fellow.

"Job done," Mixie said to herself and sniffed.

Squinting at the screen that Tilley pushed into his face, Farouk frowned, puzzled. "Is that you, Mr Gnomes, what's happening?"

A very agitated bank manager confronted the billionaire. "All monies have disappeared from your various accounts," he shouted, "and been dispersed amongst your employees, including a large amount to a person named, Kismet."

"That can't happen," whispered a terrified, Farouk, "it's not possible, is it?"

"It can, because we have a modest fully qualified genius working on your case," said Dixie, calmly.

With an oath, Farouk grabbed Kismet by the waist, produced a knife and held it to her throat.

"Hmm," said Mixie, "some action," and was by the side of Dixie in an instant and gave him a wink.

In a nanosecond, the knife flew out of Farouk's hand, and he lay on the ground groaning pleading for his mother.

Kismet staggered forward into the arms of Aladdin they fell in love immediately, married, had two point five children and lived happily ever after.

Did they? No! Of course not, that sort of thing only happens in real life.

This is what actually happened: Farouk became an honest politician and Kismet devoted her life to the poor and founded an organisation known worldwide as, Give a Lot, Gene retired to a monastery where he practiced the art of conjuring, and Aladdin started 'Lamp Makers Inc', and remained slim but saggy for the rest of his life.

***

Sometime later in a place called, Onehunga, New Zealand, a woman by the name of, Sharaz, stood in line at a Lotto shop.

When she eventually reached the counter, a purveyor of dreams, said to her, "What can I do for you?"

"Um," said Sharaz, handing over her made out card, "these numbers with random Powerball, please."

"Right," murmured the merchant of illusions as she began to process the passport to happiness. "Had any luck lately?"

"Well, yes," said Sharaz, "some time ago, I came up on the big one."

The dispenser of dreams stopped for a moment. "Really, wow how did that work out?"

Sharaz smiled, a faraway look in her eyes. "Fantastic, had an awesome experience. I ran away from a morbidly fat man and spent the lot."

"Good on you, girl, that's what it's all about," said the retailer of rainbows, with enthusiasm.

***

Meantime, back at the Villa, Mixie, Dixie and Tilley were on the sundeck, enjoying a well-earned rest after their hectic Middle East tour.

The tranquil silence was broken by, Tilley saying, "Yesterday, my parents returned from overseas."

M & D looked at each other meaningfully, with Dixie saying, "What does that mean?"

"It means," Tilley said, "that I am no longer a house sitter."

The pixies smiled, this time with Mixie saying, "Which means you will be moving into the flat under the villa."

"I thought you'd never ask," said Tilley.

They all fell about laughing.

Having listened to the conversation from under Tilley's chair, Marmalade thought… *At last, a human being to talk to.*

***

1. The author accepts responsibility for introducing a politically incorrect subject (fat) to the story of, Kismet, intending no harm to any living or deceased person.

2. The remark made by Gene to a woman whom he had just met is completely inappropriate, but unfortunately part of his character.

***

Pixiannia

Preface: The holding of a convention is an excellent concept for the dissemination of contrary information feudal bonding and confirmation the other lot have got it all wrong.

A convention is also a handy device to dodge one's responsibilities and pass decision making over to a series of groups, for example, management by committee.

This approach is also known as, kicking the problem downstairs, later, if successful to be claimed as democratic management… Perfect!

A convention then, is an all-encompassing warm blanket to snuggle in, with the primary objective of, obfuscation. CEO

***

The pixie villa sundeck was quite crowded, with four pixies, two humans a cat and two birds perched on the guttering listening to every word…

Weather wise, the day was a balmy twenty-eight degrees Celsius, which did not encourage a great deal of activity.

Mixie stretched, yawned, sniffed and said to no one in particular, "We've been thinking."

Tilley opened her eyes slowly, with a feeling of anxiety.

Gil smiled in anticipation.

Marmalade chose not to listen, but the birds did.

Fixing Mixie with a penetrating stare, Tilley said, "What do you mean by saying we? That sounds ominous."

"Us four pixies, is all," said the innocent as the day is long Mixie, with a shrug.

Sitting up slowly, while at the same time keeping a certain pixie in plain sight, Tilley made further observations. "One of you thinking is dangerous, two suicidal, but four is catastrophic."

Gil joined in by saying, "What have you been thinking about?"

Mixie's smile encompassed the whole group as she said, "We are planning a meeting." Then leaned back waiting for the splutter of fireworks.

Shifting forward in her chair, Tilley said, "Yes, come on, be more specific."

Speaking for the first time from beneath a magazine spread across his face, Dixie mumbled, "We are going to hold a convention."

Mixie smiled and left it at that.

The knot in Tilley's stomach tightened. "What sort of convention?" she asked warily.

"A pixie convention, of course," said Trixie, adjusting her sunhat to avoid Tilley's eyes.

"Yeah," grumbled Vixie, "pixie meetings are a pain in the ass, that's what I think." Then disappeared under the enormous hat she was wearing.

A silence followed Vixie's erudite announcement that could have been cut with a knife.

A thoughtful, quietly spoken Tilley, said, "How many pixies will be attending?"

"Hmm, what do you think twentyish, Dixie?" suggested Mixie.

Tilley couldn't get her head around having to deal with any more than four pixies at one time, as she sank back in the comfort and security of her cushions.

Taking a deep breath, Dixie said, "At least twenty and there could be some from across the ditch."

A faraway look took hold of Tilley at the very thought of pixie Aussie cousins…

"So where do you plan to hold this convention thingy?" asked Gil.

"You'll be pleased about this," said Mixie, with a smile. "The festivities will be held right here."

A pixie pause took place, before Tilley said, "Where is right here?"

"Under canvas and in the games room," Dixie said, "depending on numbers."

Vixie murmured from under her hat, "The pixies will be very quiet, Tilley, at night, because I'm in charge of accommodation and will make them an offer they can't refuse."

Tilley's knuckles whitened as she gripped the arms of her recliner and whispered, "Tell me, will they be similar to all of you?"

"It would be fair to say," said Dixie, "there will be some similarities, but of course, pixies are all different, just like human beings."

"Yeah," Vixie said, "apart from our Aussie cousins, they are unusual, even to us."

Tilley took a deep breath hoping for the best, but planning for the worst…

"Then, of course" – Trixie nodded thoughtfully – "don't forget our American friends, they can be a bit headstrong."

The two birds perched on the guttering looked forward to the chaos that was about to unfold.

***

A committee was formed, there always is.

At the first meeting, Tilley asked, hopefully, "What is the purpose of this convention?"

The four pixies eyeballed each other, with Mixie saying, "To have a good time and achieve next to nothing doing so."

"At last," said Tilley, with a smile, "the first honest answer that I've heard in a long time."

"Also," said Dixie, "I have drawn up an agenda that can be run up the flagpole, smothered at birth, or flushed down the toilet."

"Excellent," said Tilley, "an executive with three alternative actions, pixies like you Dixie are not easy to come by, and what about you, Trixie and Vixie?"

"We," said Vixie, "have made a list of time-consuming activities that will take the convention from boring to mind blowing stupor."

"Well done, the four of you, your executive responsibilities have not been wasted, you have minds like a time bomb with no clock and what's more, you have brought together all the elements that contribute to a successful convention." Tilley was well pleased.

The part time PA/secret agent, was, also learning how to enjoy life as a pseudo pixie…life can be seriously funny.

The dull silence after Tilley's commendation was broken by Mixie saying, "What is going to be the main theme of the convention?"

"Yes," said Dixie, "we can't hold a meeting for the sake of holding a meeting."

"Why not," observed Tilley shrewdly, "that sort of thing happens every day."

"My very point," said Dixie, "I suggest this, our main topic for breakout groups, brainstorming sessions and final plenary meeting is based upon, how can pixies be better introduced to human activities?"

"Well, absolutely fantastic," enthused Tilley, "that's all of ten minutes, what are we going to do to fill in the rest of the week?"

Leaning back with a smug smile on her face, Trixie said, "The rest of the time will be taken up with sports activities, team building rituals and gossip sessions."

Tilley nodded her head in admiration. "Yes, this is turning out to be a professionally run, measurement based, end result, dollar for dollar gigantic time-consuming exercise, well done, all of you, fantastic."

A thoughtful sense of bonding and good will enveloped the group as time was taken for reflection, broken by Dixie saying, "How do you think the neighbours will react?"

"Good point," said Tilley, "what do you think, Mixie?"

"No problem," said Mixie, "they can't even see the garden we may have to keep the noise down a bit for the party at the end of the week."

"Fat chance," said Vixie.

"Yes, well, what are some of these important activities you have planned, Trixie?" asked Tilley.

"Ah, you've got the list there, Vixie, read it out," asked the multi-millionaire.

Vixie rummaged, paper flying everywhere, reference made to her laptop. "Here it is, I knew it was…somewhere, okay, we will be having, amongst other things, football, table tennis, darts, chess, dancing, a fashion show and so on."

All agreed that the business end of any convention was the entertainment, where gossip was exchanged, rumours confirmed and reputations ruined.

The meeting was brought to a close, with all present arguing over the time and date of their next foray into organised chaos.

Everyone was pleased with how disciplined minds can ensure a seemingly simple activity ends in total disaster.

"Before we go, how much is all this going to cost?" asked Tilley.

"We have heaps of that stuff, just spend it," said Trixie.

"Too right," agreed Vixie, "we give loads to the needy and downtrodden, it's time we spoilt ourselves."

The meeting was brought to yet another close with a feeling of self-righteousness and sanctimony.

***

As one of the many meetings over the next few days came to a close, the two birds that had been perched on the sill of the open window looked at each other, she spoke first.

"This convention thingy could be fun," she twittered.

"Yes," he tweeted, "but only."

"Only what?" she twittered.

"Only, if at the end, a building burns down and there's a missing person," he tweeted.

She inclined her head in agreement. "Of course, the definition of the perfect convention, I was forgetting," she chirped.

"By the way," he twittered, "I saw that magpie the other day the one with a leg shorter than the other."

"Wow," she chirped, "that bird must have a few problems, when you think about it."

"Oh well, best get home," he tweeted, "don't want to miss the nature programme."

"What is it about?" she tweeted.

"Um…" he chirped, "something about, how to fly properly with some guy providing the background."

"Is he some kind of expert?" she twittered.

Shaking his head, he tweeted, "I don't know, never heard of him."

***

On the morning of the onslaught of the pixie horde, Tilley and Mixie were communing with nature, admiring the flora and fauna up close and personal.

As they moved around the garden, Tilley said, "You have a beautiful spot here, Mixie."

"Yeah," said the pixie, "Dixie and I tend to land on our feet after tripping over them."

Tilley smiled. "One good thing, there is plenty of outdoor space for pixies to let off steam."

There was a toot as a bus pulled in loaded with convention seekers.

As Tilley and Mixie walked towards the bus out tumbled thirty colourful, boisterous pixies and scattered immediately.

"Oh no, where's Vixie, when she's needed?" said Tilley.

Talk of the devil, the disciplinarian strolled out onto the sundeck and blew a whistle that almost burst Tilley's eardrums, bringing the pixies front and centre.

"Welcome to the Pixiannia Convention," she said. "Right, now that I've got the niceties out of the way, listen up."

Vixie then proceeded to lay down the conditions of attendance. "You lot are going to obey all my rules as I make them up, is that clear?"

"Yes!" came the shout from the gathered throng without any intention of doing so.

"Okay, we are off to a good start," Vixie said, as her eyes swept over the motley crowd.

Tilley could barely control a giggle.

"You, at the back, stop doing that It's dirty, I know you, you're from, Sydney, say no more," said the ad lib rule maker.

"Come on," said Mixie, "let's get out of here or I'll burst out laughing, and spoil the moment, they all love, Vixie."

As they left the scene, the last thing they heard from, Vixie was, "Right, now you can erect your living quarters, snap to it." And they did.

***

That evening, the committee met to hammer out final organising details, while Vixie had the attendees exercising in the games room.

And unlike human beings who react reasonably to requests for good behaviour pixies have to be threatened with dire punishments if they misbehaved.

Having settled the opening of the convention, Tilley said, "How will you handle the first session, Dixie?"

"I'm glad you asked," Dixie said, "I will present a short paper for groups to discuss, brainstorm and return to the meeting to confirm and endorse."

"Can you give us an idea about what is in your paper, Dixie," asked Tilley.

Using his laptop, Dixie looked at the group through narrowed eyes. "Pixies are not human and need to be handled accordingly when they come into existence, that is;

One, they must be kept on edge and as uncomfortable as possible,

Two, they must be kept in the dark as to what they need to accomplish,

Three, any previous experience they may have had must be ignored,

Four, interest displayed by new pixies must be stifled lest they ask for a reward,

Five, they must be kept off balance both physically and mentally."

He smiled and looked directly at Mixie, who glowed inwardly at her most favourite pixie since the invention of the plastic bag.

All present clapped, knowing the first ten minutes of the convention was going to be a success, followed immediately by the real reason for everyone's presence.

The following day, proceedings were opened by Gil and Tilley, who were advised to make their comments short and snappy, otherwise there would be stomping of feet and slow clapping of tiny hands, culminating in a phenomenon known as a pixie din.

Once the charade of the opening ceremony was over, proceedings got under way with Dixie introducing the main theme which took ten seconds.

This was followed by getting a consensus that such a topic was long overdue, five seconds.

The breakout groups and brainstorm sessions ate up a whole nine minutes, followed by a decision to adopt a pixie introduction to humanity known as, INTRO, i.e., Infiltrate – Never Apologise – Tread on Toes – Rancour – Oppression.

Some said that INTRO did appear to be a human type management concept, but then realised that humanity adhered to a much gentler philosophy, known as, 'If You Can't Beat Them Join them'.

At last, finally, to the business end of the convention, the reason for being there – let the good times roll…

The weather was playing its part – tick.

The justification crap for the convention was over – tick.

A feeling of bonhomie filled the air – tick.

The organising for the entertainment was simple with the KISS principle being used extensively.

Those interested in field sports organised their own thing. Those interested in chess ditto. Those interested in table tennis ditto. And so on. To participate in more than one event at the same time, a negotiating cudgel was introduced.

This type of organising caused, hysteria, bedlam and complete chaos, with claims it was the best of worse conventions that had ever been spawned.

Would the days that followed be memorable…yes!

Would the events be forgettable…yes!

Was the worse yet to come…yes!

What could possibly be worse?

The closing speeches of course, duh…

***

What of the events?

Yes indeed, one of the more unusual was the pixie that won the marbles and jacks competition who turned out to be a small boy.

When Tilley asked the boy where he came from, he told her he lived in a hollow tree with other pixies.

After absorbing this startling information, Tilley then enquired about his parents and was told they were both in Rehab, at which stage she promised herself to look into this sad case.

Tilley never saw the little boy again, but he saw her.

The reason the little fellow avoided his would-be benefactor was simple he didn't want to be absorbed by the Social Welfare system and spat out ever again.

The only other event worth mentioning was the best dressed pixie, female and male. Trixie had no intention of entering the fashion event instead throwing her whole being into the total disorganisation of the convention.

However, Tilley, with M & D had other plans, especially when they learned that the Australian contingent was hell bent on winning this prestigious event.

Tilley employed a top New Zealand designer in secret to create an outfit for the Chinese pixie. Came the day.

As chance would have it when lots were drawn for order of appearance, the Aussie got number one spot, whereas Trixie was last.

All of this behind-the-scenes skulduggery was unknown to Trixie, and she was still asking why she was in a competition that she wasn't in when she saw her intended outfit. She was overwhelmed, bringing a tear to her eye, which was quite a normal and sweet reaction. The impact of the Aussie contestant was enormous the list of superlatives seemed endless. The fission of fear felt by Trixie faded when she was reminded by Tilley that she had a special pixie fearless backbone. Other contestants were all of a high standard as had been anticipated, especially the Inuit entry.

Trixie strolled confidently onto the catwalk, a smile on her lips she did a twirl then continued walking, finally performing a modest pose and bowed.

A gasp came from the audience then a hesitant silence before thunderous applause burst forth, a stamping of feet, a chanting of, Trixie, Trixie, Trixie, shook the walls of the games room.

Her trouser suit of heavy red Chinese silk with Mandarin collar was other worldly; her blue high heel shoes were the exact colour of her eyes.

The only jewellery she wore were diamond earrings with random small diamonds on the side of each shoe, which caught the light as she walked.

Quite a simple outfit, really, that was the secret…

It was a no contest of course the vote for Trixie was a landslide the Aussie contingent swore a lot.

The Inuit pixie was astounded at coming in third wearing a fur hat, coat and boots, in her speech she hoped for global cooling thus saving the igloo building business in her hometown.

Oh yes, there was a male pixie Best Dressed event the next day, which everyone found very boring.

***

Now comes the pimple attached to the underbelly of the convention (don't even think about it) because there were certain conniving humans and pixies arranging a special extravaganza for the last night, which included, M & D, Gil, Tilley, Trixie and Vixie plus four musicians from the attending pixies. The rehearsals were off site and arduous. It was the evening before the last day, the games room was coping, with the general chatter being, why are we here? A small stage had been set up, the musicians assembled, some additional electronic percussion gimmicks added.

The roped off area in front of the stage raised questions among the assembled pixies.

Without any announcement or fanfare, the band, with singers, Trixie and Vixie belted out an old well known, rock and roll number.

The villa shook, with Mixie looking nervously at the ceiling and walls as a window cracked.

Then Mixie, Dixie, Tilley and Gil shimmied on the scene and performed a dance that has no name.

There was uproar unheard of in the annals of time or pixie lore.

From that opening number, the evening progressed from bedlam to tranquillity and back again.

The pixies loved it all, even Gil's corny jokes.

The final act cast a respectful veil of silence and anticipation over the audience as Mixie and Dixie danced up a storm.

Before the dance commenced, Tilley made a show of placing a piece of tissue paper between M & D and for all their whirling and twirling when the dance ended and they parted to take their bow the tissue floated gently to the floor – you can't dance any closer than that…

There was a standing ovation.

Was the evening memorable? Yes.

Were there more memories to come? Yes.

***

The day of the dreaded closing ceremony had arrived, with the captive audience restive as Tilley and Gil came on stage each clutching a bunch of papers.

A feeling of dread went through collective brains, two speeches…

Gil smiled placing at least a dozen pages on the lectern.

An ominous silence settled over the audience as hearts sank en masse. The portent for evil was abroad.

Gil smiled again, and said, "Thank you for your attendance it has been an honour and pleasure to be host to such a wonderful group."

Then he stepped back.

There was a stunned silence as Tilley came forward and said, "In the future we will be having other conventions, we look forward to your attendance, thank you."

The two then left the building as thunderous applause, stamping of feet and cheering threatened to lift the roof off.

***

To honour the convention tradition, a small papier-mâché house was burnt on the barbeque, but what of the missing person?

Well, it turned out two pixies were missing and much to the consternation of all present, Trixie and her Aussie rival, Frixie could not be found. The worse was assumed It was much later in the day after a great deal of scuttlebutt and unorganised searching that the rivals were discovered playing marbles in the back of the bus with a little boy claiming he was a pixie.

The little boy/pixie won easily.

***

The final word: As the bus rocked its way back to town with the radio belting out something groovy there were two birds sitting on the back seat:

"What did you think of the convention?" she twittered, swaying to the music.

"It's difficult to believe that anything was achieved," he chirped, thoughtfully.

She gazed through the window at the stars, thought of the morrow and worms. "It wasn't," she warbled softly.

How many times has that been said?

***

Things Past

Where to the sessions of sweet silent thought? I summon up remembrance of things past, I sigh the lack of many a thing I sought,
And with old woes new wail my dear times waste:

Then can I drown an eye, unused to flow,
For precious friends hid in deaths dateless night,
And weep a fresh love's long since cancel'd woe,
And moan the expense of many a vanished sight.

Shakespeare, William, born 26 April, 1565–died 26 April, 1616.
Bill sure did have a way with words…

***

They heard the car come swishing along the drive-in heavy rain, Tilley glad to be home.

There was a moment of silence as the garage door raised Tilley drove in, leaving the car to rest.

The door to her flat opened, she would be kicking off her shoes and putting the jug on.

"She's home," said Dixie.

Smiling, Mixie whispered, "You are a very observant pixie, just like a watchdog, in some ways."

He began to tickle her, as she squirmed away from him there came a knock at the lounge door.

"Come in if you're honest," said Mixie with the two pixies sitting at opposite ends of the couch as if butter wouldn't melt in their mouth.

Tilley poked her head around the door, she held a cup of coffee. "Got a minute," she asked.

"Sure, come on in," said Dixie, "we just finished watching, 'Meltdown' about the world going under and making a new start."

Tilley sat quietly opposite the pixies and smiled.

"Uh oh," said Mixie, "I have a feeling in my big toe Tilley has been thinking."

"Yes," said the PA/Agent, "all the way in the express lane, my speed didn't even register on the dial, giving me heaps of time to think dangerously."

"Ah yes," said Mixie, "and now you have the whole weekend to pester us."

Nodding, Tilley said, "Yes, it's truth or consequences time."

Dixie winked at his offsider. "Looks like 'fessing up time, our past is catching up with us."

With Mixie taking Tilley by surprise saying straight out, "Dixie and I were in the Pixie Regiment."

A momentary silence as thoughts flowed through Tilley's mind but came out as only one question. "How did you know I was going to start nosing into your past?"

The pixies smiled at each other, with Dixie saying, "We are very intuitive, we have practiced a lot in the past, it's like any other skill."

"Um," said a bewildered Tilley as she slumped back in her chair, followed by, "why do I get the feeling I'm going to get lost in a pixie merry go round."

She felt a funny tummy feeling as mauve and green eyes whirled in front of her...

***

Tilley listened when Mixie said, "Dixie and I have known each other professionally for years, way before we became partners."

"Yes," he explained, "we became working buddies when a special unit was set up to deal with assignments involving humans that needed help."

"You took part in our work a while back involving, Aladdin and Gene," said Mixie.

"Ah," said Tilley.

"You are aware of, Trixie and Vixie doing similar work in the community," he said.

"Oh," said Tilley.

"Then, a long time ago, we became involved in something that at the time was beyond our expertise and made a bit of a balls up of it, right Dixie?" said his offsider.

"Yeah." He nodded wisely after the act. "It involved the invisible human phenomenon known as the imagination."

"Um," said Tilley.

"We were ill prepared, not trained and didn't do our homework, leaving some humans nonplussed to say the least," explained Mixie.

"Oh," said Tilley.

"We moved from our St Heliers address to our old place getting back to carrying out assignments within our capabilities, right Dixie?"

He nodded. "Yeah, while in the meantime we resigned from the Pixie Regiment and took on work in a private capacity, much like, T & V."

"Ah," said Tilley.

"Then a while back, we were involved in a semi-disaster with the Russian Mafia as you know ending up here, how lucky for you, Tilley?" said Mixie.

"Hmm," said Tilley, unsurely.

***

Tilley found herself in bed not knowing how she got there and really none the wiser. Perhaps one day she would understand, she thought, but wasn't taking any bets on doing so. The name, Dolly, kept her awake.

That Saturday

The rain had stopped, the sun was flat out turning everything to steam it was muggy.

They all had deckchairs with a canopy sitting on the sundeck facing the driveway with a big brolly to shelter their legs.

Marmalade was under the table having been threatened with decapitation if she so much as looked at a bird.

Dixie was reading a book with the cheerful title, 'Our Days Are Numbered'.

Trolling through a dictionary was Mixie sorting out words she thought should be dumped from the English language, for example, should and if.

Tilley was thinking, before she said, "Who is Dolly?"

Pixie eyes met, with Dixie saying to his beloved, "You knew Dolly before I did."

"Hmm," said the pixie with a chequered past, "Dolly is a fully qualified registered nurse and natural healer, she's a native of South Africa, in her seventies, and rides a powerful motorbike. Why?"

Tilley shrugged. "You must have mentioned her yesterday."

"Yeah, we probably did," said Dixie, "you should also know, she lived for years over a massage parlour in, Karangahape Road and is known as, Dolly the Witch."

"Also," continued Mixie, "she is now married to someone we know as, The Author."

There was a long silence, before Tilley said, "Do you think I should continue asking questions?"

"Probably not if you value your sanity," suggested Dixie, helpfully.

Thinking of Dixie's suggestion, Tilley threw caution to the wind. "To hell with it. I want to know about Dolly and The Author."

Again, pixie eyes met with Tilley actually feeling as if they were talking to one another but there was no sound.

Looking at Tilley with a kindly smile, Mixie said, "Show her your scar, Dixie."

He pulled back his sleeve to reveal a slightly raised welt across his upper left arm.

"Oh," said Tilley, taken aback.

"That happened when we were still with the regiment, Dixie got a bravery medal." Mixie smiled at her most favourite pixie this side of kingdom come.

"Yeah, when we were still working with the, AOS," he said, "got caught in the crossfire."

"We appear to be going down a rabbit hole," said Tilley, taking a breath, "I take it Dolly was involved in the healing process."

"She was indeed, I had my arm in a sling, and by the way, Mixie has a scar, but she won't show it to anyone."

Mixie smiled. "Not in public, anyway."

"Will we ever meet, Dolly?" asked Tilley, hopefully.

Picking up her phone, Mixie worked its magic. "Hi," she said. "It's me, what are you and The Author doing tomorrow?"

She listened…listened some more…finally saying, "See you about one o'clock, Tilley our new agent, the one I told you about will make you lunch."

"I will!" A nervous chef said. "Um, uh, I don't really know about stuff like that."

"We'll help you." Dixie's smile of encouragement made Tilley even more nervous.

"Yes, later we will all go to the local store for supplies, how's that?" Mixie hit Tilley with her thousand-watt smile.

"Hmm." An uncertain frown crossed Tilley's faultless brow. "This, um, imagination thingy, why was it a balls up?"

"She's not going to let it go," said Dixie.

Another knowing, teasing smile from Mixie; "That is why we got her on our team I think it is called tenacity, one of my favourite words."

Shaking her head, Tilley said, "Why do I get the feeling I'm being, choreographed?"

"Yes, Dixie why is that?" asked his better half.

"Why is it I get the awkward questions?" he said, as they all fell about laughing.

Birds sang, glad to be alive, a butterfly appeared to flutter aimlessly, and a laden bee headed for home...

"In answer to your question, Tilley," said the only male pixie in the vicinity, "we got emotionally involved with people and that tended to become nice but messy."

He looked at Mixie, who said, "Yes, also we got into a tangle ourselves between what was imagined and reality."

Both pixies looked at Tilley, who closed her eyes, thinking then said, "Was any real harm done?"

M & D thought about that, before Mixie said, "Not really, other than there would be small gaps in memory of events, but as life kept going at breakneck speed all memory of us would just fade away."

"Apart from," said Dixie then stopped, smiling at Tilley.

"You two are just teasers," said the newly appointed chef, "come on finish me off, what?"

"Well," said Mixie, "apart from, Dolly and The Author, who came through unscathed, they know exactly who and what we are."

Marmalade stood, stretched, turned six times and settled in exactly the same spot.

"Yes, and we have a theory about that," said Dixie, "which also involves you."

Dixie's last remark caught Tilley's attention. "Oh no, what am I in for now?" she asked.

"It's only a theory, but we think the three of you have the tiniest bit of pixie in your DNA."

"Shivers, where's a mirror, quick where's a mirror?" said Tilley, as she rushed into the lounge with two giggling pixies in her wake.

She stared at a mirror which reflected a lightly tanned face that seldom saw makeup, light brown hair, brown eyes and a cute nose.

She pulled back her hair looking closely at her ears, which made the pixies laugh.

"Don't worry, Tilley, everything about you is human" – chuckled Mixie – "apart from..."

Looking from one to the other, Tilley said, "Come on you, two little buggers what is it?"

Dixie tapped Tilley's head. "Your pixie is well hidden in there, somewhere, so don't worry."

"Hmm," said the part pixie, "I feel somewhat mollified."

Throwing up her arms in delight, Mixie said, "I just love the word mollified it is so mouth-watering."

Later that day in the privacy of her own room, Mixie put a call through to Dolly. "Hi, it's me, could you bring your bike tomorrow, okay, thanks."

That Sunday

They heard it before they saw it, the deep-seated growl as the bike swept towards, Pixie Villa, followed by a more sedate quieter sedan, driven by, The Author, who wouldn't get anywhere near, the beast!

Tilley rushed onto the sundeck just in time to see Dolly's entrance, she wasn't disappointed.

Black leather one piece suit, helmet and steel capped boots, finished off with a white silk scarf, eat your heart out…

The six, including Marmalade meeting and greeting with introductions made.

Tilley found, The Author challenging, taciturn but with a quick humour, she sensed all four were, close, because of past experiences and traumas.

Dolly was shrewd, insightful, humorous and had the pixies well sussed out.

Lunch was a hoot, mainly because it was masterminded by the pixies.

Everything was 'tropical' or as exotic as the local store would allow.

It was after lunch during chatty hour two names cropped up that Tilley had not heard of previously, Fred and Emma.

Obviously, these two people had been extremely close to the pixies and were presently not in the best of health, she could see that news caused some distress to M & D.

Tilley now saw more clearly why the so called 'imagination' project had gone awry, the pixies had bonded too closely with the group involved.

Then, it was during afternoon tea, that Dolly said, "Come on, Tilley, we'll go for a spin on the, bike that other lot can follow us in the, car, you'll need to wear the spare helmet."

And so it was, the most exhilarating, smooth ride Tilley had ever had, with Dolly following all the road rules to the letter.

Upon their return to Pixie Villa, Tilley found the author browsing through Dixie's library.

"Dixie keeps himself well informed, then again, both of them do," said the author, "how are you finding the pixie way of life?"

She smiled. "You know more about them than I ever will, but having said that, would you be surprised if I said, the pixies have become an integral part of my life."

His smile reached his eyes. "They are incorrigible but endearing at the same time, they'll get under your skin, and you'll wonder what happened."

Nodding, she said, "I know exactly what you mean, and their brand of magic already has me hooked."

"You are a lost cause," he said, moving to where coffee and biscuits were being served in the dining room.

"What have you two been scheming about?" asked Dolly.

The author looked at Tilley, saying, "Shall we tell them what we were saying about them?"

"Definitely not," said Tilley, already feeling a bond forming between, the group.

***

That evening with M & D squashed in one corner of the couch, Tilley in her Penny Rocker, some west coast jazz playing quietly in the background and Marmalade curled up on the piano stool, Dixie said, "Do you want your watch back, Tilley?"

The teeny bit of a pixie glanced at her wrist. "When did you do that, more importantly, how?"

The two pixies fell about laughing, with Dixie saying, "One thing I can tell you, it wasn't magic."

"No, it was thieving," said Mixie, as a cushion came swishing through the air.

Marmalade thought... *What have I done to deserve this lot?*

***

Behind the Past

Preface: In the business of pixies helping others, at times stuff has to be made up in order to get people occupied with other things, rather than become preoccupied with their personal problems.

Pixies are extra good at making stuff up…

For example, pixies can create the impression that they are magical, when in fact they are not.

However, to be fair, pixies have physical abilities that could be mistaken for magic.

Author

***

Year: 2014. A glimpse at the pixie past

Season: Spring – summer

Time: 7 a.m. and beyond…

Mixie the pixie asked him what he was looking for, she happened to be sitting on the bathroom sink bench.

Fred looked in the mirror at the back of her head, saying, "Wrinkles," as he stretched and poked at the skin on his face.

"What are wrinkles?" she asked.

"Wrinkles," he said, "are nature's reminder."

Her eyes narrowed, she became thoughtful, before saying, "What is nature reminding you of?"

Shaking his head impatiently and looking sideways at her, he said, "Old age, that's what, something you don't have to worry about."

Continuing her interrogation, she said, "Hmm, why's that then, Fred?"

He gave her that sideways look again, saying, "Well, my understanding is that as a genus pixie do not age."

She appeared to accept Fred's explanation as he glanced to his left and much to his surprise noticed the toothpaste in its normal position.

Pixies are notoriously mischievous and her normal ploy at this time of day was to make the toothpaste disappear temporarily.

At which stage Fred would threaten to wash behind her ears, something Mixie disliked intensely, whereupon the toothpaste would reappear seemingly out of nowhere.

His suspicions aroused Fred said, "The toothpaste is where it's supposed to be what, are you up to?"

She said nothing.

So, he pressed on by saying, "What's happening?"

Her look became glum, as she murmured, "I think I've lost my magic."

To say Fred was gobsmacked is an understatement, total disbelief was closer to the truth.

Searching her eyes for a clue, Fred informed her that pixies did not go around losing their magic. Without saying another word, Mixie gave the toothpaste a narrowed eyed look and pointed her finger, nothing happened.

"There you go," she said sadly, "zip!"

Trying to reassure her, Fred explained that magic wasn't something borrowed returnable or lost.

She shrugged her shoulders drooped, as she ended her display with an exaggerated sigh.

Mixie sat there subdued, though Fred could see she had prepared herself for the day ahead, with green beret, Khaki fatigues and tan boots, standard Pixie Regiment issue.

She had made an effort despite her loss.

So, Fred started off by saying, "The best way to find lost property is to retrace one's footsteps, sort of speak."

"I don't know what you mean," she said, with a pout, "I don't do much walking."

This is true pixies have the ability to flit here and there causing a flurry of disturbed objects, much to the annoyance of Fred's cat, Burt.

Fred murmured thoughtfully, "I was speaking metaphorically about footsteps."

"That sounds awkward," she said, wrinkling her nose.

Hurriedly, Fred said, "Forget it, what have you been up to lately?"

She frowned.

"On second thoughts don't answer that," he said.

She sat there disconsolate, so Fred said, "Okay, where have you been over the last few days?"

She thought, sniffed. "I went to the Prime Minister's local office just to see what happens."

With a puzzled frown, Fred chose not to pursue that scenario, after all, he thought, what can one possibly lose in the PM's office?

Smiling pleasantly, Fred tried another possibility. "Been anywhere else in your travels?"

Now was the time to implement her plan to keep Fred occupied and not for him to dwell on the accident, so she said, "Do you think that somehow my magic ended up in the washing machine, with my dirty clothes?"

He frowned, unsure, perplexed. "I don't know anything about magic but that sounds unlikely."

"Shall we take a look," she suggested, having previously set things up.

"Okay, let's go, try anything once," he said.

They went to the back of the house, where Mixie lifted the lid to the washer, Fred peered in. "Just your grubby clothes," he said.

"What about under the top layer," she asked.

He flicked a few bits and pieces to one side.

"Look," she said excitedly, "there and there."

Peering closely, he murmured, "You mean those glittery bits and pieces, is that magic?"

"Trust me," she lied, with good intentions, "that's it, but it will need sorting and washing."

"Hmm," he said seriously, "pick out the magic bits and put it in one of my socks so it doesn't go down the gurgler."

"That sounds like a plan," she said, "but…"

"But what?" he asked.

"Well," she said, with a puzzled frown creasing her faultless brow, "how do I absorb my magic again?"

"Huh, for a pixie," he said, "you don't know much, you eat it with your cornflakes."

Continuing with her underhanded plan, she ventured, "They could be difficult to swallow."

"Jeez," said, Fred impatiently, "they'll be like any other sugar-coated cereal, crunchy as."

And so it was, they collected what Fred thought were the 'magic' bits putting them in a knotted sock to prevent machine carnage, and let it rip.

Halfway through the cycle, to keep up the pretence, Mixie demanded to see if everything was okay with her intellectual property.

She was told to put the machine on pause, peering in, Mixie wanted to know what the goo floating on top was.

Fred informed her that it looked like snot, which ended the conversation.

With the kerfuffle of the 'magic' fraud over, Mixie wanted to see how Fred would cope on his own so made a weak excuse for her absence.

***

Wandering through the empty house, Fred made his way to the bathroom, the toothpaste was in its rightful place, which for some reason made him feel sad.

Several days later, Fred was standing at the kitchen window imbibing a contemplative coffee when he noticed a movement at the edge of his vision.

Mixie settled on the sink bench, smiled and said, "Hi."

"Where have you been these last few days," he enquired, followed quickly by, "at first, I thought perhaps you'd been a figment of my imagination."

She gave a crafty kind of smile. "I've been working day and night."

He shrugged. "Huh, I didn't know pixies worked."

Her mauve eyes fixed him with a glare that made him wince. "Pixies are not bloody fairies you know, wandering around with those stick things of theirs."

"I think they are called wands," he said, weakly. "Anyway, what have you been doing?"

She softened. "When did you visit your veggie garden last?"

He sighed. "Had too much on my mind, Mixie."

Touching Fred's face gently, she said, "Yeah, I know, come on take a look, see what's happened."

The veggie patch which was sheltered behind a garden shed and couldn't be seen from the house was usually a place of contemplative peace for Fred, but not lately.

They wandered towards the back of the section Fred noticed a patch of wildflowers in full bloom that he had scattered before his world was torn apart.

As they rounded the garden shed, he was astonished at the scene before him.

The vegetable patch was now like a miniature jungle, rows of peas, runner beans, carrots and so on.

"This is amazing, Mixie," he said, as they sat on a garden seat, "you have brought it back to life again."

There was a calmness that settled over them.

They watched as bees foraged among the flowering plants, with the day pleasantly warm and the biting insects probably devouring the people next door.

"This is so nice, Mixie," he said, "thank you for coming to the aid of my garden."

She smiled, saying, "It's the least I could do after your retrieval of my magic."

They sat silently communing with nature, the warmth of the sun at Goldilocks level, as Burt hopped on Fred's lap.

Sitting there thinking of this that and the other, curiosity pricked at Fred's mind. "Mixie, about that magic of yours."

She looked at him, tilted her head to one side. "What about it?" she said, guardedly.

"How did it go down with your cornflakes?" he asked.

"Ah," she said, nodding her head.

He gave her a 'look'. "What does ah mean?"

"Well, the thing is," she started off, paused to gather her thoughts, then blurted, "I don't actually eat cornflakes."

For some 'pixie' reason, Fred had the feeling that the afternoon was going to become complicated following Mixie's ah statement.

Prodding for clarification, he said, "For want of a better word, your cornflakes appeared to disappear from the dish."

"Hmm," her answer was reluctant, "you see, I don't really need to eat anything, what you didn't notice was my sleight of hand."

"I am completely lost young lady, please explain more clearly," he asked, not giving up.

She pulled a face. "All I did was to hold the so-called bits of magic in my hand, then bingo in my pocket."

"Oh yeah," he said.

She gave him the full benefit of her enormous mauve eyes, saying, "We are talking tricks, Fred."

There was a moment of blankness as Fred's synapses went into gear, then eureka! "Magic is far-fetched and full of tricks," he shouted, smiling at his own cleverness.

"There you go," she said, patting Fred's knee for good measure.

"Okay," he said sceptically, "but what is the relevance of the speed thingy you talk about?"

"Ah," she said, profoundly.

He shook his head. "Don't start that again, Mixie."

She shrugged, looked sheepish. "Thing is, I really don't have any magic at all, Fred, so there you are."

At that very moment, she handed Fred a key.

He looked at it suspiciously. "Where did that come from?"

She smiled, saying lightly, "From next door, under the third flowerpot from the right."

"When did that happen?" he asked with a stern squint.

"A few seconds ago, to illustrate the speed thingy," she said.

He thought about her statement, saying, "But you've been here all the time."

"No, I haven't," she smirked.

"Where is the key now?" he asked, looking at his empty hand.

She shrugged, saying coyly, "I've just taken it back."

Right then, Fred gave up on the whole magic, speed shenanigans lest it overtax his brain cells.

They sat there enjoying the moment, as life meandered on its way.

She handed him an apple.

Shaking his head in amazement, he said, "You've been to the house and back and I didn't even notice."

"Yes," she said, "that is snack, remember, you need to watch your blood sugar level, and I've put the jug on and made you a sandwich, come on, it's time for a cuppa."

As he walked into to kitchen, the coffee and sandwiches were ready waiting, with Mixie watching television.

She yelled out as Fred came in, "The movies have got it all wrong, they know absolutely nothing about magic or what happened back in the day, they're not even in the zone."

"Really, what's wrong?" Fred called back, biting into a strange but nourishing sandwich.

There was indignation in her voice as she yelled, "Well, trolls get a bad press, yet under all that grunge and warts they're just misunderstood sweethearts."

"Anything else awry," he mumbled his mouth full of…something.

"Yes!" she confirmed. "Too right there is, that drongo up the beanstalk."

"You mean Jack, what about him?" Fred asked, reluctantly.

"He was a thief, caused the death of a perfectly grumpy giant," she said, in disgust.

Fred's conversation with sweet Mixie was beginning to tax his grey matter, so he said, "I'm going for a rest in the sunroom," as he grabbed his coffee and a pack of paracetamol tablets.

Settling in his favourite spot, the distant rumble of the TV assuring him of the preoccupation of his speedy pixie, Fred began to relax. Suddenly, his peace of mind was shattered by a shout as the unmistakable voice of his boarder yelled, "Whoever invented incidental music should be shot!" Then added, "Metaphorically speaking, of course."

Sweet silence at last as an unimpressed pixie turned off the TV in disgust.

***

Fred hadn't seen Mixie for some time, or, he thought, was his medication beginning to chemically take control.

He recognised that he was getting less flashback about the crash, with him walking away without any physical injury Teresa killed instantly, the drunk driver that hit them, badly injured.

He had taken a chance and purchased a dozen packets of wildflower seed which he had strewn over the newly dug vegetable patch.

Taking a well-earned break he leaned back in the garden chair, closed his eyes, but not sleeping, just listening to life passing by…

"It's going to look lovely," she murmured.

Shaking his head in disbelief, still with his eyes shut, Fred said, "Not the one and only, surely."

"Just passing," said Mixie, "thought I'd pop in."

Opening his eyes, sitting on the edge of the seat, with her legs crossed at the ankles, was a mystical creature.

They smiled at each other, her twinkling mauve eyes full of mischief.

"It's very good to see you again," was what he said and what he felt.

"Likewise," she replied, as they touched fingers.

Looking at the same, old Mixie, who hadn't changed a jot, he did note that her general appearance was somewhat dishevelled.

"So, what have you been up to?" he asked, pointedly.

"Ah," she said, "you noticed, been sorting out a gang called, The Goblins."

Taken aback, Fred's main concern was for Mixie. "What, on your own?"

She shook her head, saying, "No, no, a bunch of us pixies dealt with the kerfuffle."

He smiled. "What a sight, a pack of pixies, how charming and formidable."

A silence settled over them, just like old times as daises nodded bees hummed then a motor mower started up some distance away, heaven in the suburbs…

Eventually, looking at Fred, with a touch of sadness about her, she said, "I've got to be on my way."

He nodded. "Yes, of course, but before you go, Mixie, tell me one thing you think humankind would be totally unaware of regarding your world."

She gave considerable thought to Fred's request, before she said, "Goldilocks."

"Yes, the Goldilocks and Three Bears story, what about it?" he asked.

She smiled. "Yeah, that's the one, you may not know this, but Goldilocks was a street kid."

With a frown, he said, "I'm not with you."

"Think about it," she said, "that little sweetheart broke into a house, stole food damaged furniture and crawled into a bed not her own."

He laughed, shook his head. "We live in a crazy world, Mixie."

She looked at him with those other worldly eyes, touched the back of his hand, saying, "You mean, both our worlds are crazy."

Then she was gone.

***

Thirteen thousand one hundred and twenty-eight hours later, but still in the past…

Mixie sat on the ridge of a dormer window with her colleague, Dixie, overlooking Fred's backyard.

Night had fallen, unharmed, soundless, stars moved ever outward in the firmament, not a zephyr intruded on the scene before them.

The Italian pie party at Fred's place was well underway, with the new pizza oven proving a big hit with everyone.

"What do you think of the lighting system Fred had installed?" asked Mixie.

"Yeah," her companion nodded, "very impressive, considering the technology also keeps insects at bay, while at the same time casting a romantic blue glow over the surrounding area."

"Talking of romance what do you think?" Mixie gestured towards the laughing chattering group that were chomping on a combination of, Big Meat and More Meat pizzas.

Looking across the night, they saw Fred talking with his close friend, Emma, just far enough away from the gorging throng to enjoy a whisper or three without appearing obvious.

Trying to emulate Solomon and his wisdom, Dixie murmured, "Yes, that is a slam dunk, if I ever saw one."

"You have a way with words, Dixie, but I agree, if there was a dunk to be slammed, we're looking at it."

Smiling, Dixie said, "High fives all around, Mixie, you achieved a great outcome, considering the trauma that Fred experienced."

"Yep" – she too smiled happily – "a mixture of medication, shrink, and pixie trickery, you can't beat it, also romance can happen at any age."

"Definitely," agreed Dixie, "and come to think of it, I haven't seen Cupid for some time."

"The word on the street is," said Mixie, sotto voce, "Cupid broke his quiver in two places, but don't say I told you." She tapped the side of her nose.

Dixie's smile was bland. "I bet that brought the colour to his cheeks."

The pixies continued to watch the organised chaos of the pie party unfold before Dixie said, "So, what is our next assignment?"

"We have to call in at HQ for the details, but I think we are heading east."

Dixie thought about that vague destination, before saying, "Can you be more specific?"

Her smile was disarming. "Middle East, actually."

The look on his face was painful to see. "Oh no, sand in my underwear."

Patting his arm, she said, "Not to worry, it'll make a change."

Dixie shook his head in frustration. "I sense trouble, who do we have to rescue this time?"

"We'll confirm this, but I think it's some guy called, Gene and his cousin, Aladdin."

He thought about that, before saying, "So what's their problem?"

"The word girth was mentioned, but I'm not sure," she said.

Again, Dixie thought before saying the wrong thing. "Was the word fat mentioned?"

"Shush," she whispered, "you can't say the F word these days, you have to get with it, Dixie, big boned is now the acceptable description."

His green eyes flashed; there was despair in his voice, as Dixie muttered, "Looks like we are going to be in the land of grit for some time."

The sound of music came from pizza heaven as couples that couldn't dance, danced.

"Oh well," he said, with a look of resignation on his face, "whatever will be, will be." Then as an afterthought, he added, "Are you going to say farewell to, Fred?"

"Hmm," she said thoughtfully, "probably not, I doubt whether there would be sufficient imagination left that hasn't been overwhelmed by pie and ketchup."

"Send him a sign," suggested Dixie, "he'll know it's you."

She thought back for a moment, her early recognition that Fred needed to be kept occupied; she smiled at the toothpaste trick, the so-called missing magic, their talks in the garden and so much more over an extended period.

Making up her mind, Mixie ran a comb through her pixie hair several times creating static electricity; then, pointing the comb at Fred's latest technology caused the lights to flicker and dim.

Fred looked up quickly, waved, as he whispered in Emma's ear.

There was a moment of hesitation before Emma also gave a tentative wave to the inky blackness of the night.

Again, Mixie dimmed the lights one more time, much to the excitement of Fred's very good friend, as the guests continued consuming their long-awaited dessert as if on the verge of starvation.

Last Word

And so, we leave the past a while to view the present and the future.

***

Cooking up a Storm

Preface: When food is prepared with love all manner of indiscretions can be overlooked.
Author

***

The four were enjoying a movie in Tilley's flat, well, the romantic comedy wasn't brilliant, but at least they could pick it apart.

Marmalade was sprawled between the laps of M & D soon bringing complaints of pins and needles, whereupon, the cat would be dumped unceremoniously to circle six times and settle elsewhere, unfazed.

The movie came to an end, where the love interest, for a change, went their separate ways, causing Dixie to say, "That means a sequel, I would say."

"Will we be watching it?" asked Tilley.

Mixie twitched her nose. "Nah, dumb."

"I'm getting a coffee, and one, maybe two of those delicious biscuits you baked yesterday, Mixie," said Tilley, heading for her kitchen.

"Talking of food, Tilley, tomorrow Gil is coming to install a device that is so sensitive it can detect a mouse fart," said Mixie.

"What has that got to do with food?" asked Tilley, selecting three biscuits, not two.

"Well, Dixie and I could make lunch for you both as a surprise."

Tilley smiled, despite all the years of cohabitation with humans there were some things pixies hadn't come to understand, the tradition that a surprise was kept secret was one of them.

Settling in her chair with coffee and biscuits, Tilley said, "That discussion we had involving Fred and Emma and the, imagination fiasco, was interesting and informative, it helped me see where you guys are coming from."

"Hmm," said Mixie, "I suppose from time to time we could fill in gaps, which would help to make sense of our crazy pixie world."

"That'll be good," said Tilley, "you know, you two should start up that biscuit business again."

The pixies nodded, with Dixie saying, "What shall we watch now and criticise?"

Tilley skimmed through her DVD's. "Here's one I've always liked, 'The Invisible Foot', it's a musical."

The pixies looked at one another, with Mixie, saying, "You have the weirdest taste in movies, Tilley, put it on."

***

The next morning, Mixie began to cook up a storm…

"What are you reading?" she asked, putting the finishing touches to a pie containing four and twenty blackbirds.

Well, the pie did not actually contain birds of any size, shape or form, but there were other interesting ingredients.

Looking at Mixie from his position on top the fridge, Dixie said, "Tilley gave me this magazine and said I could bend as many page corners as I liked."

"Lucky you, what's it about?" she asked.

"Heaps," he said excitedly, "and most of it is free."

Putting a fancy edge to the pastry with a fork, she gave him her sideways look. "Oh yeah, one of those, page after page of throw away garbage."

"No, no, look here's a good one," he pointed to a full-page photograph.

She glanced at the contraption. "What is it?"

Excitedly, he said, "It's a kitchen device that peels all sorts of fruit and vegetables."

She shook her head. "Big deal, there are dozens of that sort of thing at the, Warehouse, cheaper."

"Not this one, listen up," he said, "this gadget can peel potato, carrots, parsnips, and—"

She interrupted him, "Tilley has got thingies like that, which she doesn't know how to use."

"Ah yes," he said, with a sly grin, "but can they also peel tomatoes, onions, grapes, strawberries and bananas?"

"Hmm." Her look was thoughtful, her eyes squinty. "Probably not, that gadget must cost a fortune."

"No!" said Dixie. "It's only forty-seven dollars and ninety-nine cents."

"Really," she said, slipping her pie in the oven, after checking the temperature, "what's the catch?"

"There is no catch just listen to this," he said, reading from the magazine "if you buy one, you get the second one free absolutely free."

She peered through the oven window keeping an eye on her creation. "Why would anyone need two of those things in a kitchen?"

He thought about that far reaching question for a moment, before saying, "You could give one to a friend as a gift."

"Yeah…okay, I suppose that's possible," she said, doubtfully.

"But that's not all," he said, "there's more."

She frowned and gave Dixie her full attention. "What do you mean, there's more."

The look on Dixie's face was triumphant. "Well, this is the clincher, for free absolutely free you also get three magnifying glasses."

Mixie took a precautionary peep through the oven window all was going nicely then she said, "What are you going to do with three magnifying glasses you could be running out of friends."

He nodded, a look of doubt crossing his face, then ventured. "But it's all free, absolutely free."

Sitting on the sink bench, her legs crossed at the ankles, she said, "I'm going to let you in on a secret, Dixie."

He perked up. "Really, that sounds exciting."

Looking at her partner kindly, she said, "Some people just can't resist freebies, but the only thing free in this world Dixie, is true love."

He scratched his head. "What do you mean?"

"Well, to put it briefly, all the so-called free stuff is probably in the price of the original article." She shrugged, smiled.

***

In the meantime, Gil and Tilley were relaxing on the sundeck with a cooling drink of sugarless fresh lemonade.

"Gil?"

"Yes, Tilley."

"What do you think we are likely to get for lunch?"

"Ah," he said, uncertainly.

"I don't like the sound of that ah, Gil."

"Well, I did have a meal prepared by Mixie at the embassy some time ago, and all I can say is, I'm still here," he said.

Tilley was silent for a tick tock, before she said with a worried frown, "Oh dear."

***

Meanwhile, back in the kitchen Mixie checked through the oven window, before saying, "My culinary sensation will knock their socks off."

"I'll get all the eating devices," he said.

"Yes, okay, Dixie, and don't forget the salt and pepper," she emphasised.

He shook his head. "I've never seen them use it."

"I know, but Tilley always insists that condiments be put on the table otherwise it looks naked."

Whilst Dixie busied himself with his duties, Mixie with oven cloth rampant carried her epicurean delight placing it on a large silver tray then the pixies made their way to the sundeck.

As Mixie placed the tray on the table, Tilley took a deep breath. "Your pie smells delightful, but I can't quite identify what it is yet."

Gil nodded enthusiastically. "Yes, a lovely aroma and it looks sensational with the crimped edges, very artistic."

Mixie glowed with pride as Dixie basked in the reflected glory.

"You do the honours, Tilley," said Gil.

Taking a knife presented to her by Dixie, Tilley cut into the pie, saying, "This pastry, Mixie, is cooked to perfection and cuts without crumbling, fantastic, you must show me how you achieve that."

Instead of glowing, the praise this time made Mixie tingle all over.

Taking her first bite, Gil watched for Tilley's reaction as a look of surprise crossed her face. "This…this pie, Mixie, is superb, I've never tasted anything like it."

As Gil got stuck in, he was unable to agree because his mouth was too full for comment.

Sometime later after having seconds, Tilley said, "You have to tell us the secret Mixie to this culinary delight."

The chef's smile was coy her manner humble, as she said, "Most everything in that pie came from the fridge."

"Come on," encouraged Tilley, "share your culinary expertise, we're all family here, including Marmalade, who I see has turned up."

"Want some pie?" said Dixie, offering a small piece to the cat.

Marmalade sniffed the proffered tidbit her ears flattened as she beat a hasty retreat.

"Take no notice," said Gil, "what does she know."

Mixie sat on the corner of the table her legs crossed at the ankles. "Let me see, for starters I prepared the pastry then put it aside to breathe."

"How very professional," said Tilley, "what happened next?"

"Um," thinking back, Mixie said, "we found some kumara, washed and divided it into pieces, but didn't peel it."

The first worried frown crossed Tilley's brow.

"Then," continued Mixie, "came the onions, we washed them but left the stringy bits because a lot of good food is wasted by humans."

Tilley's frown deepened.

"Keep going," said Gil, enjoying the moment.

"Okay, while I was doing that, Dixie put the kumara in the oven with some olive oil and a dusting of cinnamon." Mixie smiled knowingly.

This information made Tilley's eyebrows shoot up. "Cinnamon, how interesting," she said, despite her misgivings.

Mixie turned to her offsider. "What happened next?"

Dixie thought for a moment. "Let me see, that's right, we diced the onions, caramelised them and chucked in a dessert spoon of mustard powder."

"Yes," said Mixie picking up the thread, "it was then that we found some strawberries."

Gil said hopefully, "Are we getting dessert as well?"

"No, no," said the chef, "the strawberries are part of the pie ingredients."

"That's right," continued Dixie, "the strawberries were thrown in with the onions both absorbing each other's juices."

Tilley's eyes closed.

"Correct," said Mixie, getting into the swing of things, "then came the piece-de-resistance we discovered two chocolate fish at the back of the fridge."

With this announcement, Tilley's hands gripped the arms of her chair as her knuckles whitened.

With a thoughtful look at Tilley, Gil said, "I wonder what Christmas they were from." Tilley's eyes remained closed.

"Yes, I must say we did have a few problems with the fish," said Mixie, "the chocolate was okay because it melted quickly, but that pink stuff inside refused to melt then Dixie had a brilliant idea."

Tilley's eyes opened slowly, then without menace she said, "And what was that idea, Mixie?"

"Well," said the cookery wizard, "he suggested the pink stuff be popped in the microwave."

"Yes," said Dixie proudly, "that pink stuff surrendered immediately and turned into a glutinous jelly."

"That's right," said the chef, picking up the story, "there was a bit of spitting and popping until we put the pink stuff together with the strawberries and onions in that enormous frying pan your mother gave you, Tilley."

Dixie smiled, as he got into the story. "That was the stage we added the diced kumara with the juice of two lemons and a banana."

Tilley looked into the half distance and sank lower in her chair.

"Are you okay, Tilley?" Gil asked.

With an airy wave of her hand, Tilley said, "I'm fine, just fine why would I be anything else but fine?"

Picking up the threads of the story, Mixie said, "Anyway, to cut a long story short, I lined the pie dish with pastry, threw in all our prepared stuff, put the top on then chucked it in the oven."

A peaceful silence enveloped the group, until Dixie said, "We are so pleased you liked the pie."

Dixie's statement was followed by a short reverential moment before Tilley said, with a tear in her eye, "These two idiots are just sweethearts," as the words of the author echoed in her head, 'You are a lost cause'.

The two kitchen hands basked in Tilley's approbation for several seconds before Mixie said, "There is one more thing, I suggest that you stay away from our kitchen for a while."

"Yes," Dixie explained, "there is, um, some cleaning up to do, which could take time."

Mixie nodded. "Yes, it's the pink stuff on the ceiling which could prove to be a problem and we may need professional help."

Gil got up from his chair, stretched, burped, apologised then added, "Well, I have to get back to the embassy, thanks for a great lunch and the entertainment."

"Yes," said Tilley, "I think a nap will be in order after such a gourmet experience."

Last word:

The pixies are cooks mythological

The setting was pleasant

The company delightful

The ingredients apart couldn't be faulted

The combination of parts was challenging

The proof of the pudding was in the eating (proverb, author unknown)

The diners were unscathed but left wondering.

The Game of Life

By: Mixie & Dixie.

    Mixie: I think it's long overdue.

    Dixie: I happen to be watching a good movie.

    Mixie: What is it?

    Dixie: The Intermittent Monster, what's overdue?

    Mixie: Writing our own story.

    Dixie: Just a sec let me hit pause… What, us actually putting pen to paper, sort of.

    Mixie: Yes, writing our own stuff.

    Dixie: What is our story going to be about?

    Mixie: Something controversial.

    Dixie: Now you're talking, such as?

    Mixie: Um, well, accepting the premise that life is a game of chance, who do we think will survive in the long term, the good or bad people?

    Dixie: Do we assume that the so-called good people decide which is which?

    Mixie: Yeah well, don't let us get too technical, but thinking along those lines, Dixie, just who are these so-called bad people?

    Dixie: That's easy, anyone who has a different point of view than oneself is either bad, wrong or both.

    Mixie: That sounds reasonable.

    Dixie: How about this for a thought, nature will win in the end.

    Mixie: That is sound reasoning, because even the mighty dinosaurs couldn't beat a natural phenomenon.

    Dixie: Yes, and I wonder if some global warming can be attributed to the dinosaurs?

Mixie: More than likely, when one thinks of their bowel movements compared to their size.

Dixie: I agree, after all, life came from a chance combination of water, chemicals and Goldilocks heat, so nature itself contributed to GW back in the day, and don't forget the volcanoes.

Mixie: Another point to consider, Dixie, is that life is cyclical.

Dixie: What, going around in circles?

Mixie: I know many humans that go around in circles.

Dixie: Not ever decreasing ones, I hope.

Mixie: Hopefully not, because we all know what happens to them.

Dixie: Yes, well we won't dwell on that.

Mixie: Okay, so far so good, now let's assume for a moment that not anything lasts forever, perhaps this whole life thingy will start again, but next time instead of a Big Bang explosion there will be a Big Bang implosion.

Dixie: Brilliant thinking Mixie that is definitely hypothesising outside the square, Albert and Stephen would be impressed with your intuitive and controversial theory.

Mixie: So, would that mean instead of heat, water and chemicals, there would be exactly the opposite, cold, dampness and dross?

Dixie: More than likely, because the circumstances would be exactly opposite, everything would exist inside out.

Mixie: Fantastic! I think we've cracked the crap question that many people ask ad nauseam, what is life all about?

Dixie: You are absolutely right, Mixie, life rolls on relentlessly, despite human endeavours to foul their own nest and quicken the process.

Mixie: Working that out was easier than I thought it was going to be.

Dixie: Yeah, and I had better hit play again because the monster is just about to bite a family's collective heads off.

Mixie: Oh good, I want to watch that part.

Dixie: We should check our theory with Tilley in due course.

Mixie: Yes, because with her PhD she will know if we are on the right track.

Dixie: Oh look, what's happened.

Mixie: The monster has spit out all the heads, the wrong flavour do you suppose?

Dixie: Monsters aren't like they used to be.

Mixie: Even monsters have to be politically correct these days, Dixie.

Dixie: Yeah, perhaps the heads were the wrong shape I give up even thinking about it.

***

Lockdown the Virus

Preface: Like the dinosaurs we are told collected a king size hit from a natural disaster, will the beginning of the end for *Homo sapiens* be slow in comparison and sneaky?

Will life ever be the same brought about by the magic of a quintessence that will mask the unpleasant taste of doomsday?

Or are the answers to these questions in the offing tantalisingly out of reach?

Take a breather, humanity and enjoy the view while you can.

Author

They were sitting at the table in Tilley's kitchen, when she said, "So, it's going to be us four for the duration of our incarceration."

Under the table, Marmalade thought... *I wonder if being incarcerated interferes with, my feeding arrangements?*

"Ah," said, Dixie, thoughtfully.

"Hmm," muttered Mixie, with a frown.

"Why is it I sense complications from an, ah and an hmm?" murmured Tilley.

"Yes, Dixie, why is that?" asked Mixie.

He fielded the question with aplomb, looking at Tilley with a faint smile on his lips, he said, "Because your maths is slightly out of kilter."

Very seldom having her sums questioned, Tilley merely raised an eyebrow which was sufficient for Dixie to say, "Trixie and Vixie, as we speak, are winging their way towards us."

A spasm of uneasiness went through, Marmalade, as she thought... *That means four pixies within these four walls for at least a month.*

Dixie's remark caused Tilley to say, "That means four pixies within these four walls for at least a month, that scenario causes me to have misgivings."

"Ah yes," said Mixie, with assurance, "but remember, Tilley, you have a spark of pixie in your DNA which means only a minor imbalance in your equilibrium over that period."

"I'm unsure if your explanation makes me feel any better, Mixie," said the part time pixie, as the thud of an embassy helicopter got too close for comfort coming into land on the grass in front of Pixie Villa.

"As you would expect, Trixie and Vixie arrive in style," said Dixie.

The group, including, Marmalade rushed to the sun deck, in time to see the two pixies alight from their transport with, Vixie, hanging on to her gigantic hat with both hands.

Then the whirly bird was gone.

Sitting around the table once again, Trixie said, "You realise, Tilley, that pixies are immune to the dreaded Lergy, we are here to support you through the ordeal of isolation."

Marmalade thought… *What about me?*

With Vixie saying, unsurely, "Cats are also immune, um, I think."

"Who is going to be in charge of our pastimes so that we don't kill each other?" Dixie asked.

Three pairs of pixie eyes, one set of human eyes and feline peepers settled on Vixie, with Tilley saying, "The best one among us for that job is, our very own taskmaster."

The disciplinarian narrowed her eyes, saying, "Come with me you shower." Leading the way to the games room, she continued, "Name something we can do together."

"Table tennis," said Dixie, "and darts."

"You, Dixie will organise games for those two," directed Vixie, "anyone else?"

"Um, ten pin bowling and quoits," ventured Tilley, a tad unsurely.

"They will be your responsibility," said Vixie.

"We have all sorts of board games," said Mixie, "I'll sort them out."

Vixie looked at Trixie, with a keen eye. "I'll organise the pool table and rowing contraption."

"And I, with Marmalade," said Vixie, "will be in charge of the assault course, please have your plan with me by lunch time, dismissed."

And that's what happened, plus baking biscuits, Tilley reading a potted history of M & D's exploits which she found amongst Dixie's books and dealing with a gang of bozos. Ah yes, the bozos.

The pixies were having a quiet game of poker in Vixie's room, Tilley tinkling on the piano when she heard the sound of a car.

She made her way to the sundeck looking down on a large black rough as guts clapped out old bomb in which were four occupants.

Tilley sensed a problem knowing the pixies would have picked up the arrival of their visitors.

Stall for time was her first thought.

Four large men, all dressed in black alighted, looking around with calculating, shifty eyes.

The bozo with a dilapidated trilby on the back of his head looked up at Tilley, saying, "We are here to take your stuff."

With a charming smile, Tilley said, "Ah yes, you must be here to collect that pile of horse shit out the back, it won't all go in the boot, you know."

"Cheeky bitch," said the one with his hat on backwards, "she'll regret that."

"What makes you say that?" said a voice from behind the men.

En masse, they whirled around to see, nothing.

"Where did that come from?" asked the one with the crutch of his trousers level with his knees.

"From over here," said another voice, somewhere off to the left.

The gang of four turned, to see, nothing.

"What the hell is going on?" This came from the intellectual member of the group.

"Up here," said Vixie, from the roof.

Four heads whipped up to see a small creature that said, "Keep them covered if they twitch fire at will."

"It would pay you not to move until you are told," said Tilley, politely, as the sound of a police siren could be heard coming along the drive.

"Lay face down," Vixie said with her best growl, "because fingers are itching."

As the police car pulled up, all they saw was a woman on a sundeck looking down on four prone figures.

Afterword:

Disease desperate grown by desperate appliance are relieved or not at all. Shakespeare Lockdown meanders with hope in mind April 2020.

***

The police recorded the incident for training purposes, and called it, 'Diversion Tactics'.

***

Ingram Content Group UK Ltd.
Milton Keynes UK
UKHW020629140723
425126UK00003B/27